Midwinter Nightingale

Books by Joan Aiken

for Young Readers

Midwinter Nightingale

JOAN AIKEN

Delacorte Press

Published by
Delacorte Press
an imprint of
Random House Children's Books
a division of Random House, Inc.
New York

Visit us on the Web! www.randomhouse.com/kids
Educators and librarians, for a variety of teaching tools,
visit us at www.randomhouse.com/teachers

Library of Congress Cataloging-in-Publication Data
Aiken, Joan.
Midwinter nightingale / Joan Aiken.
p. cm.
Summary: The Wolves Chronicles continues as Dido and her friend
Simon, Duke of Battersea, have many perilous adventures trying to
protect the ailing King James from the plotting of the evil Baron
Magnus, who is determined that his brutish son Lothar will be the
next king of England.
ISBN 0-385-73081-0 (trade) — ISBN 0-385-90103-8 (lib. bdg.)
[1. Adventure and adventurers — Fiction. 2. England — Fiction.]
I. Title.
PZ7.A2695 Mk 2003
[Fic] — dc21
2002031350

The text of this book is set in 12.4-point Cochin.

Book design by Marci Senders

Printed in the United States of America

June 2003

10 9 8 7 6 5 4 3 2 1

BVG

foreword

AFTER THE SHOUTING and furious language, and the turmoil as the helmeted men with pikes and pistols left, dragging his father with them, a shocked silence fell inside the house.

His mother sat at her rosewood desk with her head propped on her hands, staring at nothing. She looked like an image carved out of salt. Mara the nurse tiptoed and pottered about, offering wine, cider, hot posset, but was sent downstairs to the kitchen. Neither woman took any notice of Lothar, huddled in his corner.

After a while there came the sound of horses' hooves outside, and carriage wheels. Lothar raised his head. "Did they make a mistake? Are they bringing him back again?"

"Of course not."

Her voice was no more than a cobweb of sound. And

no wonder, after all the savage names that had been hurled at her.

"Who can it be?"

"It will be Frank Carsluith."

Lothar pushed out his lower lip and scowled. "Why does *he* have to come here? Stuttering and fussing and fidgeting? I don't like him."

"He comes with a message from the king."

Lothar's underlip stuck out even farther.

"My lord Viscount Carsluith," announced the nurse. A tall, willowy figure followed her into the room where they were sitting and swept off his plumed hat, revealing a fuzz of silvery fair hair. He glanced round the room and its disordered furniture with a gloomy nod.

"Shall I bring refreshments, Lady Adelaide?" asked the nurse.

"No, leave us. . . ."

Mara looked round for Lothar, but he had hidden himself behind an overturned settle.

"My poor dear," said Carsluith. He crossed the room and kissed Lady Adelaide's hand. "Was it very bad?"

"Worse than I can say! He cursed me—in *such* a way. . . . Do you think the curses of—of somebody like that—do you think that they *matter*?"

"No, no, no, of course not!" But Carsluith rather spoiled the effect of this reassurance by making the sign against the evil eye and then asking, "What exactly did he threaten?"

"Oh, I don't want to think about it."

2

"No—forget it. Think about something better. Your marriage to Baron Magnus is formally annulled. The archbishop of Westminster has set his seal to the deed of annulment as from yesterday. You are completely free."

"Free," she repeated in a wondering, dazed tone.

"And His Majesty sends a message. He is happy to permit your marriage to Prince Richard of Wales—indeed he—he does not command, but he *begs* that the marriage may take place as soon as possible. And I think you are well acquainted with the prince's feelings on the matter—"

"Yes," she said faintly.

"They suggest that the ceremony should take place at Clarion Wells cathedral next week."

"So soon?"

"It cannot be too soon for the prince's wishes. He is preparing a residence for you at Haymarket Palace."

"And this house? Fogrum Hall?"

"Whatever you wish shall be done with this house, Adelaide. It can have no happy memories for you. It could be pulled down."

"I will consider." Infusing a little more strength into her threadlike voice, she asked, "And the children?"

"*Children?*" Carsluith sounded thoroughly startled.

"Lot—my boy—the son of Magnus—he is five—"

"I'll be six in three weeks," corrected Lothar sulkily, scrambling out of his hiding place. Carsluith made only a very slight attempt to disguise his surprise, distaste and disapproval at the discovery of the boy's presence in the

3

room, but good breeding and good nature came to the rescue.

"Good heavens, young fellow, I had no idea at all that you were here! You must be very happy that our good, kind Prince Richard wishes to marry your mamma. He will be your new father. And a—" He cut himself short.

"Will Mamma be queen, then, when old King James has died?" demanded Lothar.

"Yes, she will," responded Carsluith, after a slight, astonished hesitation. Gad, he thought, the boy's a chip off the old block. We shall have to watch this one. We shall certainly have trouble with him.

"And when my new father Richard dies, shall *I* be king?"

"No, my boy."

"*Why not?*"

"Because you are not the king's son. My lord Richard of Wales already has a son, Prince Davie, by his first wife, who died. He is the prince of Cumbria. You will be friends with him, I am sure. But, Lady Adelaide, I believe you mentioned *children*?"

"Yes," she answered in a troubled tone. "I understand that Zoe Coldacre had a baby girl who will now be a few months old—Zoe died in childbirth, you may not know—the sister of my nurse, Mara, has charge of the infant, for Zoe's family cast her off—Magnus took no interest in her, but he did not deny that the child was his— I believe she is called Jorinda—"

4

"She is hardly *your* responsibility," objected Carsluith.

"But, poor child, if I do not undertake the charge of her, what will become of her? And she is Lot's sister, after all."

More of that bad blood to worry about, thought Carsluith, but King Jamie is a shrewd old party; he will soon have the problem sorted. Perhaps he can send the brats off to the Colonies. And—thank goodness—their father is safe behind bars for the next fifteen years.

"When shall I see my *proper* father?" Lothar wanted to know. "Why did those men take him away? Where has he gone?"

"He is gone to the Tower of London."

"How long will he be there?"

"Fifteen years," said Carsluith in a tone from which he could not banish very considerable satisfaction.

"Is that a prison?"

"Yes."

"Why? What did he do that was wrong?"

"You are too young to be told about it. Your father has—a kind of disease—a mixture of sickness and wickedness; he killed several people. Perhaps—it is hoped—he can be cured of his malady while he is confined in prison."

"*Why* does he have to be shut up?" his son asked again.

"I told you. Because he does harm to people."

"I don't *want* him to be in prison," Lothar whined, and

slammed his fist on a mahogany table so hard that blood spurted from his knuckles. The two adults stared at him in shock and dismay.

"Lot," said his mother faintly, "go down to Mara and tell her that I said you could have a burnt-sugar frumenty."

"I don't want one."

"Run along, now—like a good boy."

"Why?"

"Because your mother says so," snapped Carsluith.

"Oh, very well." He went out, dragging his feet.

"When Richard and I are married, he will soon settle down," said Adelaide, but she said it without conviction.

"King James will know how to deal with him," agreed Carsluith in the same doubtful tone. He added, "Now that the boy is out of the way, I can give you this." And he extracted a small jewel-studded box from his pocket.

This, when opened, proved to contain a ring, set with an enormous rose diamond. Lady Adelaide gazed at it through tear-filled eyes. The huge stone swelled, glittered, seemed to cover the whole space ahead of her.

But Carsluith was thinking: There's bound to be trouble ahead. With those children, with that background . . .

chapter one

THE WETLANDS EXPRESS was notorious for running well behind schedule, and today the passengers
could see that it was going to be even later than usual by
the time it reached Distance Edge Junction. Here the
train was due to divide in half, a passenger coach and
four freight cars turning south to Windfall Clumps,
while the main part continued westward toward the
Combe country, the mountains and the sea.

Simon, looking out the rain-streaked window into the
creeping landscape, began to fear that dark would have
fallen by the time he reached his destination. He was
bound for a solitary manor house situated in a wilderness known as the Devil's Playground because its thickets and swampy woods and overgrown hedgerows were
so tangled and mazelike that travelers had been known

to get lost among them and wander in circles for days on end.

Rain splashed down the dirty glass, blurring the view of soggy meadows and waterlogged woodlands. Then — quite unexpectedly — the train jerked to a stop. Peering out, Simon saw that they had come to a tiny wayside halt; he could just make out the words FROG MERE on the single signboard. In the long pause that followed, nothing could be heard but the slap of rain on the roof and a deep sigh from the engine, as if the train were expressing its intention of never moving again.

But then the silence was broken by the slam of a door. Somebody — astonishingly in such a godforsaken spot — somebody had entered or left the train. Now footsteps came clacking in a purposeful way along the corridor, and the door to Simon's compartment was vigorously slid open.

Simon sighed, almost as deeply as the train. He was not at all anxious for company.

The girl who came in gave him an intent, considering look, half frowning, half friendly, before settling herself in the diagonal corner with a swish and flounce of dark brown velvet skirts and a twitch of her long fur driving coat. She neatly aligned her feet in well-polished boots and then, when she had made herself thoroughly comfortable, gave Simon another long, shrewd scrutiny.

"You look human, anyway!" she remarked. "Really, when a person travels across this country, they hardly know what to expect. I've been told there's still marsh men with webbed feet! So I do like to pick a compartment where there's somebody who at least looks as if he would know what to do if the train broke down."

Simon was doubtful whether he deserved this compliment. And he was not at all flattered by her wish to join him. The errand that brought him to this wild secluded country was a particularly private one and he wanted no hint of its nature to leak out. But he had a kind heart and did not like to snub the girl who had chosen his company.

He had to admit that she looked inoffensive enough. Her hair was dark and short and curved close about her head under a fur cap. Her round freckled face was not pretty—her pink cheeks were too plump, her nose and mouth too big—but she looked lively and keen, dimples showed in her cheeks and a pair of dark gray eyes laughed at Simon as she settled a foreign-looking cat in a cage on the seat beside her.

"I won't eat you, I promise! And nor will Malkin here, will you, puss? I can see that you are wishing me at the world's end. But I swear that I am really very harmless. I'll even guarantee not to talk at all if you prefer silence. But if you *like* to talk—as I do—my name is Jorinda."

"Mine is Simon."

As soon as he had said this, Simon wished he had held his tongue. But the name did not seem to strike any chord in Jorinda, who, taking this as an acceptance of her offer to chat, went on doing so in a low husky confiding voice with a hint of a chuckle in it.

"You see, it is like this: My brother has finished school—at least, he was dismissed for bad behavior—if the truth be told—so I decided that I might as well quit my own abode of instruction in Bath (where they quite washed their hands of me in any case; they say I am incapable of grasping anything beyond ABC) so as to be back at Granda's manor before news about my brother reaches him—and so cushion the blow for the old boy. Don't you think that is best? Don't you think it a sensible plan?"

"Will your grandfather be very angry with your brother?"

"Oh, yes! Prodigiously! The last time Lot was expelled, Granda had a seizure, and foamed at the mouth, and Dr. Fribble had to bleed him and cauterize and phlebotomize him and put him to bed for three weeks with cold compresses and antiphlogistine and nettle gin—that was after Granda had chased Lot round the stable with a walrus tusk and knocked out two of Lot's front teeth. One trouble is, you see, that Lot is only my half brother; he isn't Granda's grandson. Granda never really wanted to have us wished on him. He was only persuaded by Lord Hatchery, who is our cousin and Master of Foxhounds."

"Is your brother younger than you?"

She shook her head.

Simon thought she looked rather old to be still at school. Seventeen or eighteen, perhaps? He wondered why she spoke of her grandfather and not her father or mother—where were they? But he was not really interested in her confidences and decided that this would be a good moment, while the train was at a standstill, to walk along to the horse box and check on the well-being of his mare, Magpie.

"I'm just going to visit my mare," he said to the girl. "I'll be back in a few minutes." He stood up.

But Jorinda had already plunged into an account of how her brother, who was the cleverest person she knew, had been sent to school at Fogrum Hall after being thrown out of Harrow.

"He has never been able to spell, you see—that's the trouble—as often as not he can't even spell his own name—so teachers think he is stupid, and that makes him *so* angry. Because, you see, he is not stupid—not in the very least. He has *wonderful* ideas—about how to run the world—sometimes the things he says are quite amazing. Why are you standing up? Sit down again directly!"

"I'm going to see my—"

But the girl swept Simon's objection aside. She grabbed his hand as he moved across the carriage intending to edge past her and step out the narrow doorway into the corridor, and gave it such a jerk that, without intending to, he sat down on the seat opposite her.

"That's better!" She laughed at him. Her face, Simon thought, was very like that of a squirrel, with round cheeks and slightly protruding teeth and large bright eyes.

"Are you hungry?" she went on. "My maid will bring

in a picnic by and by. After we have gone through customs. Where does that happen?"

"At Windwillow."

"*Customs!* What a stupid business that is! Who ever could have thought it up? And why? When my pa and ma were young you could travel anywhere, all over the country, without these stupid stops and payments—so my old nurse has told me. Why should I be obliged to pay a tax to these customs officers if I take my Granda a present of Shrewsbury cakes or Bath biscuits or Pontefract licorice pipe tobacco?"

"It came into force when the country was split up into four different kingdoms," Simon explained, "when the North country and the Combe country and the Wetlands all declared independence from London."

"Oh, I know; I know *that*," she said pettishly. "But still I don't see why these stupid rules should apply to people like *us*. . . . It is all very well for farmers and drovers, I daresay. Why, even—" She stopped and bit her lip. "Forgot what I was going to say! Anyway, politics are dull and idiotic—ain't they? Stuff only fit for old graybeards. In fact I think this country—north, south, east or west—is detestably dull—don't you? But when the old king finally pops off—as he's supposed to do soon—they say everything will be different. Do you think that is true?"

"I really can't say," Simon answered carefully. "When King James died and King Richard came to the throne, I don't remember there being much difference."

"Ah, but then, King Dick was old Jim Three's son. They were as like each other as two peas in a pod. But now, nobody seems quite sure who the next king will be, which makes it more exciting—don't it? When my pa comes out of jail—"

She stopped and clapped a hand over her mouth. Her expression was horrified, but her eyes laughed at Simon.

"Oh, *mercy*, what have I been and gone and let out now? My brother Lot is always saying that my tongue will be my downfall one of these days! Forget what I said, will you, pray?"

"Of course," said Simon politely. "Anyway, people can be sent to prison for all kinds of reasons—" not necessarily criminal ones, he was going on to add, but the girl interrupted him.

"My pa's reason was lycanthropy—and that's not really his *fault,* after all. I don't think people should blame him and send him to prison for a failing he was born with—do you? You might as well be sent to jail for having measles. It is wholly unfair! Of course, at the time, there was a lot of trouble. In fact Grandma died of the disgrace. That was when Lot and I were quite little—fifteen years ago—so we don't remember her. Nor Pa, for that matter. He's been in jail for nearly all of my life."

"I'm sorry," Simon said, wondering what lycanthropy was. He had never heard the word. Illegal swinging on lych-gates? Licking ants' nests? Forced entry into liquor stores?

13

But the girl was chattering on. "Of course Granda never liked our pa; I've ever so many times heard him say, 'Why m'daughter was so besotted as to go and marry a perditioned werewolf chap I'll never comprehend,' and our old nurse has told me, time and again, that Granda was against the marriage from the very start — though our pa does come from a very grand old ancient family in Midsylvania. . . . But, as I told you, what's so unfair is that Pa can't help it. So it's really no fault of his. He was furious when they put him in the Tower for fifteen years. Said he'd get even with them all when he came out. Still, he may have changed his ideas while he was inside. Don't you think? People do, so they say. . . ."

"I believe I have heard of your father," Simon said cautiously. "Is he Baron Magnus Rudh?"

"Why, yes."

The engine sighed again, then let out a loud moan, as if it suffered from acute stomach cramps. The whole train jerked backward — forward — backward again, amid a chorus of men's shouts, loud clanks and hammer blows.

"They must be adding some more coaches," Simon said. "I have never known them to do it here before."

"Why, do you often travel on this line?"

"No, not often." I am no good at this kind of secret, diplomatic business, Simon thought. I wish I were back minding geese in the forest. Or painting in my studio. But painting is what I have been summoned for. Well, I wish that Magpie and I were safe at Darkwater Farm.

Now a loud bleating, which Simon had been half consciously noticing for the past five minutes, became even louder, quite deafening, as if a hundred sheep had climbed onto the train and were finding themselves seats in the next carriage.

"We seem to have a flock of sheep on board," he said, changing the subject.

"Oh, I saw them in a siding when I got on," Jorinda agreed carelessly. "A couple of stock cars loaded with them. They will be going to market in Windlebury, I daresay."

She sounded supremely uninterested.

"Well, while they are attaching the sheep, I shall go and take a look at my mare," Simon said firmly, putting on his coat, and this time, instead of walking along the corridor, he left the carriage on the platform side and walked back, through the pelting rain, to the horse box at the rear of the train. Now there were three stock cars behind it, which had been shunted from a siding.

The horse box, Simon had observed when Magpie was led on board at the London terminus, was of a far superior construction to the passenger cars, which were old and shabby, with cracked windows and worn upholstery leaking straw at the split seams. The horse box, in contrast, was magnificently fitted up. It must at some time have formed part of a royal train. There were polished mahogany stalls lined with thick cotton padding, each with a coat of arms on the door, brass mangers that glittered like gold, deep trays filled with sand for the horses to stand in and ingenious water troughs filled by a drip from silver tanks overhead so as to avoid too much spillage. Huge bales of hay lined the coach so that the equine passengers need never go hungry.

Magpie seemed content and was quietly chomping on a nose bag of oats that Simon had left for her. She greeted him with a friendly snuffle and rubbed her head vigorously on his chest, then returned to her meal.

"Good ol' gal, ain't she?" said the horse-box attendant, a wizened little man with a brown face like a withered oak leaf. "Lucky, piebalds are reckoned—ain't they? Windfall Clumps, that where you and she's bound for?"

"That's right." Simon pulled out his and the mare's tickets, one pink, one green, and the man clipped them. He said, "But you have to go through customs first, at Windwillow. Anything to declare?"

"Only my paints and paintbrushes and the mare's bag of oats. And two saddlebags."

"Arr! Those be the very kind of baggage they go through fiercest—like a mouse in a lardy cake," the attendant said, absently brushing off a mouse that had run up his gaitered leg (the horse car was alive with mice because of all the spilled oats).

"Why?" Simon asked.

"Why! Word has it they be a-looking for a lost piece o' joolry—Queen Adelaide's crown. Mind—no one never tells *me* nothing. Maybe 'tis Princess Sophronisba's choker customs gentry be after, but I dunno—'tis all fancy and make-believe, I daresay, so's they can claim extra wages—" and he spat between the hooves of a dapple-gray pony who was occupying the stall next to Magpie's.

"Where are the sheep going?" Simon asked. A sudden surge of bleating came from the car next door as it was shunted into place.

"*I* dunno. Like I said, no one tells *me* nothing. Mind, I did hear as they was going to Burgundy—but I reckon 'twas a Banbury tale."

"Burgundy? But that's across the Channel! And—" Simon was going on to say, we are almost at war with Burgundy—but at that moment the engine gave a loud authoritative whistle and there was a violent jerk as the new couplings were tested.

"I'd better get back to my seat," Simon said, then gave the old man a guinea and ran back along the corridor to his own compartment.

The glass-paned door was half open and he saw the girl, his fellow traveler, reflected in it as he approached. She was standing up and had opened the door of her cat's travel cage. The cat, Simon had noticed before, was a most unusual and foreign-looking beast, pinkish cream in color with very soft, thick-looking fur and black points, ears, paws and tail. It seemed well accustomed to travel, sat very composed, bolt upright, and gazed into space with a lofty air, ignoring everything outside its cage. Now its owner pulled from her pocket a small notebook or pamphlet and very quickly and neatly slid it under the pink velvet cushion on which the cat was sitting. The cat took no notice of this. Then Jorinda closed and locked the cage, attached the key to her ear—Simon had noticed before that she wore silver earrings shaped like keys—and sat down nimbly in her corner seat.

As Simon entered the carriage she looked up at him, smiled and said, "Was your mare quite comfortable? And my pony? Ah, thank goodness, we are starting at last—I have been *so* bored, sitting here with nothing to look at but those damp bushes!"

Simon wondered very much what the booklet that Jorinda had hidden under her cat might be. Vaguely he remembered hearing that there was a very heavy tax on the export of certain kinds of books and written material from one part of the country to another—or was it forbidden altogether? I'll have to find out more about that kind of thing, he thought dismally; sometime it may be my job to know all about such laws. This was a prospect he did not look forward to at all. In the meantime he felt that it was none of his business if the girl intended to smuggle a forbidden paper through customs—if she wanted to risk being fined or imprisoned, that was her own affair.

Plainly unaware that he had seen what she had done, she continued to chatter cheerfully about her school, and her brother, and what her father might do when he came out of prison.

"It must have been a great chance for Pa to read and

study—I daresay he will be very well informed when we see him next," she said primly.

"Will he be coming to your grandfather's house?" Simon asked.

"Mercy, no! Granda would have another seizure! No, no, I daresay he will go to friends . . . ," Jorinda said vaguely. "He has bought a house, I believe. . . ." Then she suddenly let out an ear-piercing scream, startling Simon almost to death.

"*Oh! Oh!* Oooooooooh! Help! Help!"

"What on earth is the matter?" he asked impatiently—he was rather bored by the girl and could see no cause for the terror that seemed to have seized her.

"There! *There!* On your coat—there! Oh, if it comes near me I shall die, I know I shall!"

She jumped up on the seat, whimpering, sobbing, laughing and gibbering hysterically.

Simon was wearing a long caped riding coat of gray duffle. Looking down at it, he saw a large mouse run swiftly along the hem and vanish into a fold of the material.

"A mouse? Is that what all the fuss is about? It must have climbed onto my coat when I was in the horse box. There are dozens of them along there. It's nothing to be scared of."

"I can't bear them, I can't *bear* them!" she cried hysterically. "If it comes near me, I shall faint, I shall die, I know I shall!"

19

What a carry-on, Simon thought, about one little mouse. His opinion of the girl, which had never been particularly high, shot down. But he twitched aside a fold of his coat, was lucky enough to spot the mouse and grabbed it by its tail.

"Ugh! Ooooahh! How *can* you?" said Jorinda, shuddering and shutting her eyes.

Simon had half a notion of offering the mouse to the cat—but the cat, sitting with eyes closed, seemed supremely uninterested in what was going on; anyway, it looked overfed. Instead Simon opened the window and tossed the mouse out into a beech coppice through which the train was now passing. On a thick carpet of dead leaves the landing should be soft enough, he thought.

Next minute he felt the train begin to brake and slow down.

"I think we are coming to Windwillow, where they do the customs inspection," he said. "I'll have to go back to the horse box; my saddlebags are there."

"*Please* don't bring back any more mice! My maid will see to my luggage before she brings the lunch," Jorinda said.

How boring to be a rich girl and obliged to travel about with a maid, Simon thought, though he supposed it must be convenient in some ways. He grinned a little, thinking of his friend Dido, who had made her way all over the world without any help but her own wits.

The bleating of the sheep was almost unbearably loud

as he reached the horse-box door. Just beyond this, trestle barriers had been set up across the station platform,
and a sign saying NO PASSENGERS PAST THIS POINT.
PLEASE TAKE YOUR LUGGAGE TO THE CUSTOMS INSPEC-
TION COUNTER AT THE END OF THE STATION.

Simon climbed into the horse box, lifted down his saddlebags from the brass hook where they were hanging
and unstrapped Magpie's nose bag. This seemed oddly
heavy, considering how few oats were left in it, so, wondering if a stone or some undesirable object had found
its way into the feed, he thrust his hand inside, sifted
through the grain and chaff with his fingers and was not
altogether surprised to come across what felt like a piece
of string connecting some hard lumpy objects the size of
grapes; when he pulled this out, it proved to be a necklace of green stones on a silver chain. Simon frowned a
little over this find and glanced toward the attendant,
who was ostentatiously occupied polishing mangers at
the far end of the horse box with his back turned. Since
this man was the only person who could have dropped
the necklace into the nose bag, which Simon had filled
after the train started, there was no point in questioning
him, for his reply was bound to be a lie. Instead Simon
calmly hung the necklace on a nearby harness hook. He
then very slowly and deliberately searched through the
contents of his saddlebags, which held paints, warm
clothes, some packets of raisins, a tube of spillikins, and
a small magnetic chess set. Frowning a little over this,
Simon dug down to the very bottom of the bag and

21

found a velvet box lined with goose down and containing a diamond clip. The diamonds were magnificent ones, as big as peas.

"No, really," muttered Simon crossly. "This is too much. What do they take me for, a Hatton Garden salesman?"

He perched the little box on a traveling anvil that stood nearby, then finished his search of the second bag, but found no more alien objects. The old attendant, who had been watching him for the past few minutes, nodded gloomily.

"Arr, thee's got a bit of sense in thy noddle, young feller, simmingly! Customs gentry do be devilish keen to turn in a-plenty smuggled goods; don't they dig out any theirselves, they baint above planting a few gewgaws in folkses bags so's to claim finder's fee—" and he scowled at the brooch on the anvil.

"So I see," said Simon dryly, rather regretting the guinea he had given the little man earlier, and he went once more carefully through his luggage and pockets before walking along the platform to where the customs officials were waiting, with unconcealed impatience, behind a wooden counter.

"Took your time, didn't you?" one of them grumbled. "Come on—pass over the bags—we haven't got all day."

Simon saw a thin elderly woman struggling onto the train with several heavy bags. He guessed she was Jorinda's maid. She and Simon seemed to be the only passengers, unless other people had passed through the customs turnstile while he had been in the horse box. And what about Jorinda? Had she some special exemption? Or had she and the cat passed through before the maid and the luggage?

The customs officers—two redheaded lantern-jawed men with hair cut so short it looked like rusty paint over their bald heads—seemed seriously displeased about something. They searched through Simon's belongings again and again, strewing his clothes about on the trestle table, poking suspiciously inside his paint pots, prodding a skewer through a cake of soap, spilling raisins on the station platform.

"Hey!" Simon protested. "My things are getting all wet."

The men ignored him. "We was told, definite, they would be there," one of them muttered to the other.

"Go through the chap's pockets again."

They went through Simon's pockets; they made him take off his riding boots and delved inside. Finally—sourly and with great reluctance—they let him repack his scattered belongings and get back onto the train.

By the time Simon finally returned to his own carriage, he found that the elderly woman was there with Jorinda, unpacking a hamper that contained a lavish picnic—game pie, simnel cake, roast chestnuts, crystallized grapes, ham patties, cheese, hard-boiled eggs and apples.

The elderly woman, who was very sour-faced, threw Simon a glance of dislike, suspicion and warning. This did not surprise him as much as the exceedingly warm welcome he received from the girl, who jumped up, gave him a radiant smile and looked as if, had they been alone, she would have flung her arms round him.

"My lady! Sit down at once!" snapped the maid. "Young ladies don't rise when a male person comes in. *Never!*"

Jorinda blushed deeply; her eyes met Simon's in a deep, grave, sparkling look that filled him with embarrassment and discomfort. What has got into the girl? he wondered.

"Oh, but he's my kind friend, Nurse Mara!" she said in an urgent, throbbing tone. "He saved me from a mouse!"

"That was nothing at all," Simon said quickly. "All I did was throw it out the window. Did you have any problems with the customs?" he added, feeling rather uncomfortable, as they were all three standing in the small space between the seats, and he would have liked to sit down and take out the roll he had brought for his lunch.

Nurse Mara sniffed, as if she too thought rescue from a mouse nothing out of the common. "Your ladyship is just *silly* about mice," she remarked, and repeated, "Sit down, do, child."

With a swish of skirts Jorinda reseated herself and gestured for Simon to do so too.

"Won't you *please* share my picnic?" she begged, and fixed him once more with that deep, meaningful, glowing gaze. "For I shall never be able to eat it all by myself."

Good heavens, thought Simon uneasily, anybody would think the girl had fallen in love with me. But we have only just met!

"Th-thank you!" he stammered. "But—but what about this lady?" He turned to look at Mara, who was snappishly unfolding a starched napkin.

"Oh, she is only a servant." Jorinda coolly took up a slice of game pie and bit a large semicircle from it. "*She* takes her tiffin in the baggage car. You need not bother your head about *her*. Not in the very least."

Nurse Mara fixed Simon with a basilisk stare that emphatically contradicted these words.

"Do please have some of my picnic," Jorinda repeated, munching. "The game pie's not bad."

"I won't, really, thank you," Simon said, rather awkwardly seating himself in what space was left from the feast. "As a matter of fact I don't eat meat."

"*Don't* you? Why? How very queer! Well then, have a hard-boiled egg—do! Or some chestnuts."

Jorinda went on pressing him until at last, to pacify her, he took an apple and bit into it. At the crunch a tawny owl, which had been asleep in the rack for the past hour, woke, opened huge round eyes, let out a snoring sound and clicked its beak.

Jorinda gave a sharp cry. "What's *that*?"

"It's only my owl. Thunderbolt. He won't hurt you. He likes to sleep all day."

Jorinda's cat, which had opened large plum-colored eyes at the sound of the owl's voice, shut them again, as if the interruption was too trifling to be worth his attention.

Nurse Mara shrugged furiously in a gesture that said, "What did I tell you?" and left the compartment. But, evidently placing no trust whatsoever in her young mistress, she continually came back to do some small thing: open a pot of jelly, peel an egg for Jorinda, or just glance sharply through the glass door to make certain nobody was misbehaving. And soon she came back to repack the remains of the picnic lunch and warn her charge that the next stop, Distance Edge, was where they had to get off.

"My granda's manor is about twenty miles from there," Jorinda told Simon. "Sir Thomas Coldacre, of Wan Hope Height. Where are you bound?"

Her face fell when he told her that he was going south to Windfall Clumps.

"Oh! What a pity! I hoped you were traveling my way. Shall I give you my address? Will you give me yours? As a matter of fact I haven't quite made up my mind . . ."

Simon hurriedly explained that he did not know what his address would be—that he would not, probably, in any case, stay there for very long—would shortly be returning to London—his plans were uncertain—all depending on other people.

Jorinda's face fell even more at this, but brightened a little at the mention of London.

26

"*I* mean to go there as soon as Granda will let me. Papa has a house there. London's a fine town, ain't it? But I do, I *do* wish for us to meet again. We *must*!" Her fingers clutched his arm. Simon looked anxiously toward the door—but Nurse Mara was out of view for the moment. "What is your address in London? We could meet there—please—couldn't we?" She fixed imploring eyes on his.

What a queer girl, thought Simon. All those years at school, you'd think she'd be a bit cooler in her manners.

He decided that he had no option but to tell a lie, a thing that went much against his nature.

"Oh, I shall probably be staying with my aunt Bessie in—in Hans Town."

"What is her direction? Her surname?" Jorinda pulled out an ivory tablet.

"Mrs. Nettlepink—18 Prince Richard Row," said Simon, hastily inventing.

By this time the train had jerked to a halt.

"Come along—do, my lady," urged Nurse Mara, "Your grandpa's coach will be waiting. And besides, we've—" Her last instruction was drowned in a tremendous outbreak of baaing from the sheep as if their state had become much worse—more, suddenly, than they could bear.

Petulantly, Jorinda snatched up her cat in its cage and followed the nurse, turning, as she stepped down onto the platform, for a final beseeching look at Simon.

Knowing that it would take at least five or ten minutes

for the train to be divided and the two parts to go their separate ways, Simon waited a moment or two, until Jorinda and her nurse ought to have left the station, before stepping out to make sure that his own compartment and the horse box were correctly positioned in the part of the train that would turn south to Windfall Clumps. What was his surprise, then, to see that Jorinda was still on the platform, much farther back, toward the rear, beyond the horse box, in earnest confabulation with a grimy-looking man who was leaning on a long pole. She handed him something—money, perhaps— then, without noticing Simon, turned and followed Nurse Mara through a wicket onto the road beyond, where a chaise drawn by four horses waited. Two men followed, heavily burdened down with luggage.

Simon stayed where he was until the carriage began to move; then he walked along to the horse box. Behind him he could hear shouts as men uncoupled the first four coaches that would continue westward to the Combe country. At the rear of the train a second engine was huffing into position to push the stock cars and a single passenger compartment south to Windfall Clumps and Marshport.

Now Simon saw the reason for all the bleating he had been hearing for the past hour, and he was appalled.

Three cattle coaches had been hitched on behind the horse box and they all held sheep. But the coaches were not solid wooden cars—they were merely topless cages constructed from thin metal bars, each about twice the height of a man; and the sheep had been stuffed into them quite regardless of the poor animals' comfort, so that the ones on the floor of the cage were being crushed by the others piled on top of them. Each cage was crammed to its fullest capacity, and the top layer of sheep in each cage was held down by a tight net.

The ones at the bottom must soon be suffocated, thought Simon in horror. Indeed he saw that one poor beast, on the floor of the car, had been so desperate for air that she had thrust her head between two of the iron cage bars, buckling them and almost decapitating herself in her struggle to get some breath into her lungs.

Simon was filled with such fury and outrage at this sight that he strode along to the engine and said to the driver, who was helping another man connect its coupling to the cattle cars, "Whose sheep are these?"

The driver turned and looked at Simon in mild astonishment. "Blest if I know, guvner! We gotta take 'em to Marshport—that's all *I* know."

"Well, who does know?"

"That feller as loaded 'em and traveled here along of 'em. Where is he? He was along there a minute ago. He left his crook—here it is, a-leaning against the waybill."

Simon recognized the staff of the grimy man who had talked to Jorinda. But of the man himself there was no sign.

"How did he bring the sheep?"

"Drove 'em onto the platform, guvner, an' hoisted 'em into the trucks. There was only just room. He had a dog, a handy clever brute that one were, kept the wethers rounded up."

But the man and his dog had gone; though he searched all over the small station, Simon found no sign of them.

Returning to the engine driver and his mate, who were looking at him in mild amazement, Simon said, "This is disgraceful! There are laws forbidding such ill-treatment of animals."

"Arr. So there oughter be! *But,* who's about to see they're kept?" said the driver, and his mate nodded gloomily and spat.

"Well, *I'm* going to, now, this minute. I'm going to let those poor beasts out."

"Eh! Ye canna do that!" The driver was scandalized.

"Can't I though?" Simon took the pole that the sheep-herder had left behind and, with it, unhooked a couple of latches that kept the side of the sheep cage in position. It folded down to make a sloping ramp onto the platform, and the sheep tumbled and spilled down it, bleating and staggering, some of them hardly able to move, bewildered, gasping and trembling. A few of them continued to lie motionless on the floor of the cage. For them the rescue had come too late.

"Blimey!" said the engine driver. "That's showing 'em, though, ain't it?"

"But look here," said his mate. "They sheep do be somebody's property. We had to deliver 'em to a Mister Mitchle Bone at Marshport. What's he a-going to say about this howdydo? Or Sir Thomas, what they come from?"

"Tell him to get in touch with me and *I'll* pay him (if he dares to, knowing how those poor beasts have been ill-treated)." By now Simon had undone the fastenings of the second and third sheep cars and more and more of the liberated animals had tottered down to the platform and the rail track.

"Here's my card," said Simon, handing a pasteboard square to the driver, and he repeated, "Tell the owner to get in touch with me."

"But guvner—what be ye a-going to *do* with all they dentical sheep?"

Simon had climbed into the horse box and now reappeared, leading Magpie with her saddle, saddlebags and bridle strapped on.

"Do?" he asked, tightening a girth. "Why, I'll take them to where they can get better treatment."

"Not on our train?"

"Certainly not on your train. They can do the journey on foot. But it's not far."

"Reckon they'll follow ye, guvner?"

"I reckon so," Simon said with confidence. "Animals mostly do." He put two fingers in his mouth and let out a piercing whistle.

Some of the sheep, who had started to nibble on what sparse vegetation there was around the station, lifted their heads and moved toward him. Thunderbolt the owl came drifting from the open carriage window. Simon jumped up on Magpie's back and Thunderbolt settled on his shoulder.

31

"Come up, mare! No more train travel."

Magpie, not sorry to leave the stuffy horse box, shook her head and whinnied, then trotted off briskly alongside the rail track that led south. Simon whistled again, and the whole flock of sheep streamed after him in a gray-white mass.

"Well, by gar!" said the train driver. "Us mit as well go home for the day; there's no other passengers on this part of the train."

"What about me?" grumbled a peevish voice. It was the horse-box attendant, standing on his steps.

"You can wait for the two-thirty-five back to King's Cross."

The driver was studying Simon's card. "By gar!" he said again. "Who'd a thought it? Proper well set up young un he were, but no more than a lad, I'd ha' said. But looky here. . . ."

"Why? Who is he then?" asked his mate, staring at the card. "I'm no scholard."

On the card in black capital letters were the words:

SIMON 6TH DUKE OF BATTERSEA

"He's a blooming dook, that's who he be," said the driver.

The chaise, which had been stationary all this time behind a clump of willows, now proceeded on its way.

chapter two

THE TOWER Of London was not a pleasant place in the best of weather, and on a damp, dark, foggy winter evening it was at its worst. The massive masonry was blackened by tendrils of wet moss, peacocks let out doleful cries from the aviary, the lions roared despairingly from the menagerie, and they were answered by the long-drawn angry howls of hungry wolves on the Kent side of the river Thames.

Dr. Blisland, though he had entered the gloomy fortress on every day of his life, in his official capacity as fortress physician to any prisoners who might require medical attention, felt an unaccustomed shiver in his spine that evening as he climbed the slope to the Traitors' Gate and walked toward the Wakefield Tower, where his patient was confined, passing a sign that said ADMISSION TO HIS MAJESTIE'S VIVARIUM OF WILDE

BEASTES 6d. Another, opposite, said HEARKENING CHAM-
BER. WEREWOLF HOWLING 9d. Two large sacks, presum-
ably containing 6d and 3d pieces, reposed outside these
doors. They were corded up and sealed with red wax,
ready to be taken to the Bank of England.

The guards nodded as Dr. Blisland passed by; they
knew him too well to require a sight of his pass.

"How is the baron tonight? At all wrought up?
Feverish in any way? Expectant?"

The armed guard who stood with his harquebus at the
foot of the winding stair shook his head. "Not that one,
sir. Cool as a carrot. You'd think he'd be just as glad to
stay in as to be let loose. You'd reckon he'd been here fifteen days, not fifteen years."

Dr. Blisland shivered again as he climbed the worn
stone steps. Fifteen years in this place! he thought.
Enough, you'd guess, to finish off someone with the
healthiest constitution, let alone one with such a strange,
terrible complaint. . . .

"No tantrums? No high strikes?" the doctor softly
asked the second guard, who stood whistling a carefree
tune at the top of the stair outside the massive iron-
barred door. He shook his head.

"Not a chirp or a squeak. Mild as a mudpat. Calm as a
cowslip. Didn't even want to look at the evening paper."

The guard nodded to a sheet that lay beside him on the
step. The headline, in huge black capitals, read: "WILD
BEAST marquis out at last. 15-yr term completed.

Queen Adelaide's ex-husband to be released tomorrow. Baron who swore revenge now walks free."

The guard chuckled as he turned the huge key and shot back several bolts.

"In fact the gentleman said he'd sadly miss your evening parley-vouz — the port wine and the pill."

"Let us devoutly hope that he continues taking the pill," the doctor said, a trifle uneasily. "Does he plan to return to his London mansion — Armorica House? I could continue to pay a daily visit there."

"No, I fancy he plans to spend but one night in town and then go on to Fogrum Hall. His son is there, you know, Master Lot."

"Yes, I do know." The doctor frowned, then shrugged. "Nothing we can do if the man chooses to associate with that worthless boy."

As the guard slid back a fourth bolt, the two men heard a low-voiced call from within.

"Excuse me one moment, pray! I am at my devotions."

"Take as long as you like, my dear sir," the doctor returned heartily.

Respecting the silence that ensued, the two men retired a step or two down the winding stair and continued their whispered conversation.

"Mighty strange to think that man was once married to Queen Adelaide."

The guard shook his head in agreement. "But she was only a young lass in her teens at that time, Princess of

Thurinia, remember—came from one o' they Euro-lingian families where the gals get no say as to who they marries. Good ol' King Jim, he unfastened the knot quick enough as soon as he knew what she had to put up with."

"Assisted by His Grace the archbishop."

"Ay, to be sure. His Holy Nibs undid the buckle in double-quick time."

"I wonder, though," said the doctor thoughtfully, "where that leaves the *son* of that marriage. . . . Does he inherit his father's title?"

"No loss if he don't, I reckon. By all accounts he's a proper young blayguard. Was that a true tale about the peacocks he—"

"Hush! I hear Baron Magnus calling!"

A faint voice could now be heard inside the door.

"Are you there, my dear sir? Now I am *quite* at your service and shall be most happy to welcome you to my poor abode."

"And I am ready for *you*, my dear Baron!" the doctor exclaimed, springing up the stairway. The guard followed him, whistling cheerfully, undid the last bolt and pushed open the heavy door, which opened inward. As the doctor stepped in, a skinny hand shot out from behind the door and seized his wrist in a grip of steel. He let out a startled cry.

"*Aha!* My dear sir! I fooled you finely—finely—did I not?"

The grip was at once relaxed; the baron stepped from

behind the door, revealing himself as a frail-looking elderly man with snowy white locks which, in prison fashion, he wore loose to his shoulders. He was not above middle height, but so thin he seemed taller. He wore a suit of rich black velvet and his white shirt was of the finest cambric. His face wore at all times a look of immense mildness and innocence, replaced only very rarely—as now—by a twist of puckish humor.

"There—there! It was too bad of me to put you in a fright! On our last evening too! I believe you really thought I had returned to the bad old days. Did you not? When I had to be held down by eight men before you could oblige me to take the pill. Never fear, my dear Doctor! Those times are gone beyond recall. Now I can hardly remember them without abhorrence. Why, nowadays I welcome the pill with gratitude—with fervor!"

The doctor had in fact been badly startled, and it took him a minute to recover.

"Shall I stay, sir?" suggested the guard, a trifle uneasily.

"No, my good man, that will not be necessary," Baron Magnus told him with a patient smile.

But the guard kept his eye on the doctor, who finally gave him a nod.

The man withdrew, but murmured, "I'll be right outside, Doctor, if you should want me. . . . Just give a call." And, when outside the closed door, he recommenced whistling, to show that he was within earshot.

Baron Magnus frowned, shrugged, murmured,

37

"Odious, odious noise! Repulsive tune! I wonder if he is aware how much I hate all tunes? *Perhaps* not . . . But the poor fellow means no harm, I feel *almost* certain. . . ." And he moved toward the table, while the doctor, opening his bag, withdrew a small phial, containing one white pill, and a silver flask, from which he poured a portion of port wine into a glass that stood ready for him.

The cell occupied by Baron Magnus was wedge-shaped, accommodated to the round tower that contained it. The furnishings were simple — a bed, a table, two chairs and a curtain across one corner, where toilet things were housed. Meagre light from two small slit windows high up was augmented by many candles. The dark stone walls were hung with rich tapestries embroidered with forests where wolves, stags and huntsmen endlessly pursued one another among many-branched trees. Costly carpets covered the floor.

"How piercingly sad this is!" sighed the baron, reseating himself at the table. "How very, *very* much I shall miss our evening conferences, my dear doctor! They have furnished the gladsome summit of each day. And yet, my good friend," he added, as the doctor approached him with the glass of port in one hand and the pill, a very large one, held between finger and thumb, in the other, "yet, my dear doctor, my days passed in this unsought, unplanned seclusion have not been wasted — far from it." He pointed to a massive pile of leather-bound volumes stacked against the wall.

"All these works have been imbibed, absorbed, committed to memory. I emerge from custody a far wiser, better-informed being than the sad, resentful fellow who first reluctantly entered this melancholy edifice. I shall have so much to impart to my dear wife—ah—forgive me!" he said, as the doctor, startled, spilled a splash of port wine on the tablecloth. "Allow me!" The baron pulled a snowy kerchief from his pocket and wiped away the drop of wine. In doing so he accidentally flicked the pill that Dr. Blisland was proffering. It fell on the carpet.

"Forgive me!" the baron exclaimed again, and bent from his chair to retrieve the pill. "Here it is, quite safe! I shall swallow it forthwith." He did so. "And now I shall imbibe this superlative wine, which I suspect, my dear sir, is furnished from your own cellar—am I not right? I do not believe that the prison medical service would ever supply such a superior vintage. But I seem to have surprised you, dear Dr. Blisland? What can I have said that caused you so to start?"

"It—it was just—" stammered the doctor, greatly embarrassed, "it was just that—has Your Excellency forgotten that Lady Adelaide—er—passed away some years ago?"

And was married to the king at the time, he might also have said, but did not.

"Ah, yes, indeed. Indeed. This prison solitude inculcates a certain slowness of wit, a grievous lethargy of memory. Of *course* my poor dear Adelaide died some time ago—a most unfortunate occurrence, was it not? Now I begin to recall the circumstances. Something fell

39

on her from above, did it not, as she was attending divine service?"

"Er—yes—that is so," replied the doctor, deciding to pass over the fact that when she died, the Lady Adelaide had been married to King Richard IV for some years and was queen of England. Poor thing, she's dead anyway, so he can't harm her now, supposing he should wish to, he thought, remembering the baron's litany of screaming, raving denunciations and threats as he was dragged from the courtroom.

"I shall gnaw their vitals! I shall chew their tongues. I shall pull off their fingers and use them for bookmarkers; I shall dangle their bodies in my moat for the pike to finish off. I shall make them sorry they ever saw my face!"

His own distorted face had been almost unrecognizable as he shouted these threats; suffused with hate and fury, he had looked more like a wild beast than a human being.

How remarkably different from the way he appears now, thought the doctor, studying the baron's gentle, smiling countenance. What a wonderful effect those pills have had on him, to be sure! I shall write an article for the *British Medical Journal,* he decided, recorking the empty port flask, about the beneficial effects on L.A.D., Lycanthropy-Aggravated Dementia, of Saint-Peter's-wort with evening primrose and rose of Sharon imbibed daily with a moderate dose of vintage port wine. Why, at one time, that man who now sits, so gentle, sensible and chatty, across the table from me, at one time he actually believed, and would have others believe, that he was a . . .

"Poor, *poor* Adelaide," sighed the baron, picking up his glass and inspecting it, to make sure there was no drop of wine remaining. "How greatly she must be missed. But I shall be overjoyed to embrace our dear son, Lothar—I am sure he resembles his beloved mother. I am very sure he will be a comfort to his poor widowed father."

That he won't, thought the doctor uncharitably.

He stood up.

"Well, Baron, this is goodbye, then? Unless you plan to remain in town and should wish to avail yourself of my services at any future time?"

"No, no, my dear friend, I am for Great Distance and Fogrum. But—should I at any time return to the metropolis—I shall take it as an act of friendship if you will dine with me at Armorica House?" He showed his very white teeth in a beguiling smile as he said this.

"A safe journey home to you, then."

"Dear me! The dwellers on the South Bank seem uneasy tonight, do they not? Something appears to be troubling them. I wonder what it can be?"

"It is the winter cold, I daresay," said the doctor, with another shiver. "The lions in their cages are accustomed to warmer climates—"

"But the wild wolves are of a hardier temper," the baron said, smiling again. "This cold weather stirs them up to sing for their supper. I like to hear them at it! I shall miss their nightly anthem when I quit these quarters, hospitable in that respect if in none other. No, dear Doctor, I do you an injustice. *You* have always been a kindly host with your healing medicine and your agreeable talk. *That* I shall also miss. What a contrast to my royal cousin Richard, who has paid no single visit in fifteen years." A single malignant flash came and went in his dark eyes.

"Er—I—I believe he was instructed by his councillors of state—" the doctor said, stammering slightly.

"Doubtless, doubtless. But now I must delay you no longer. Adieu, my dear sir."

He made the doctor such a deep and courtly bow that he seemed unaware of the hand extended by Blisland, who, after a moment's hesitation, bowed likewise and then tapped on the door in the prearranged signal for the guard to let him out.

"Evening, your lordship," called the guard through the doorway as he let out the doctor. "Me and Sam'll bring up your supper in a brace of shakes."

"Pray do not trouble yourself, my good man," returned the baron in his gentle voice. "I do not wish for any supper. I do not find myself at all hungry."

"Oh? Very good, sir—if you say so." Having shot the bolts, the guard clattered away down the stair, whistling as he went. A frown of vexation darkened the baron's face, and the yellow light gleamed momentarily in his eyes.

"That tune again! Always that idiotic tune he whistles. But not for much longer . . ."

Crossing his cell, the baron stood before one of the figures in the tapestry, a huntsman engaged in drawing his bow. He was life-sized, and the two pouches he wore, doubtless intended for game or weapons, had been cunningly unstitched at the top so as to render them capable of holding real articles. Into one of these the baron dropped a pill that he had concealed in his kerchief. The bag already held several hundred pills.

"There, my dear, dear, dear friend," murmured the baron. "There goes the last of your offerings. Now we shall see what we shall see."

Downstairs the gatekeeper gave an irritable kick to the two heavy sacks of silver coins that were still impeding the passageway.

"Why don't those sorbent treasury messengers come when they're supposed to? *Now* what am I to do? I have to lock the outer gate and those sacks'll be underfoot all night. Here, you, Anderson, take and put them up on the roof, will you? They'll be safe enough up there, the gulls and ravens won't swipe 'em and the messengers 'ull be justly served that they have to go the extra distance in the morning."

"What, me? Carry those heavy sacks up all those stairs? Who do you think I am? Hector Herculoosoe?"

"Go on, man, you don't have to take them both together. Make two trips of it."

Still grumbling profusely, the assistant guard did as he

43

was ordered. The heavy sacks chinked and jingled as he struggled with them up the winding stairway.

When he came back after depositing the second one by the roof parapet, he said, "There! I hope you're satisfied. It's pouring cats and dogs, enough to melt the seals and rot the sacking. Why people want to pay good money to see some peacocks and hear wolves howling, blow me if I know! And now I'm going off duty."

Upstairs in his pie-shaped cell, the baron rubbed his hands slowly and lingeringly together, then sat down to wait out the last twelve hours of his fifteen years' imprisonment. His pale face was unmoving and inexpressive as marble, but his eyes shone like molten steel.

• • •

Two small tugs, *Smith* and *Jones*, were guiding His Majesty's ship *Philomela* through the sandbanks and shallows of the Thames estuary on a dark and foggy winter night, when they were intercepted by a rowing boat that shone a blue light.

"*Philomela* ahoy!" shouted a voice.

"Rot and sink you!" grumbled the master of *Smith*. "What's all this? Piracy in London River?"

"No, there's a civilian passenger aboard *Philomela* that's urgently wanted by His Holy Nibs."

"Ah, and how do we know that's a true tale, not just Banbury sauce?"

"I've a password."

"Let's hear it, then."

"Lower a dinghy. Can't go bawling passwords over nine yards of Thames water."

"That's so."

The message was thus relayed and the password whispered: "Pendragon."

"That'll do," said *Philomela*, satisfied. "Who's the passenger that's wanted?"

"Young female by the name of Dido Twite."

"We'll drop her over the side, then."

After a short interval, this was done. The passenger, a small dark figure, with her baggage, was deposited in the rowing boat, which pulled rapidly away for the Essex shore. And the ship with its convoy proceeded upriver.

"So why do I have to be off-loaded in this mirsky capsy way in the dead o' night without a word's warning?" grumbled Miss Dido Twite as two dim blue lights on the Essex coastline drew closer.

"Can't tell you that, ma'am. But there's a fellow ashore will soon make all plain."

This promise was not immediately kept. A light curricle with a driver and one passenger and two impatient horses waited at the rear of the landing stage, which was situated on a dark, deserted stretch of marshy riverbank. The moment Dido and her small bag had been bundled into the carriage, the driver cracked his whip and the horses set off at a gallop.

But even in the dark Dido had recognized her fellow passenger. His height and bulk were unmistakable.

"Podge! Podge Greenaway! What's all the mystery about?"

"His Holy Nibs will tell you that. I better not go spilling any beans," said Podge. "For the matter o' that, I've not many to spill. 'Tis all to do with a pal of yours painting a picture. That's all *I* know."

"Painting a picture? Croopus! Does that mean that Sim — ?"

"Whisht, gal! Walls have ears, and so do hedges. All I know is that a message came to me and Dad, asking where was you. And all we knew was that you'd gone to visit friends in New England but was expected back sometime around Christmas."

"That's so," agreed Dido. "And I hitched a ride back with my pal Captain Hughes on his frigate. I been visiting my friends Nate Pardon and Dutiful Penitence on Nantucket Island. And why the pize shouldn't I do that?"

"No reason on earth why you shouldn't," said Podge. "But there's been a heap of different kinds of trouble a-brewing up here — I can't tell you more about that, but His Reverence will — and there's a big question that nobody can answer — except, seems you might be able to."

"A question?" Dido was really puzzled. "Is it about S — ?"

"Hush up, dearie! We better not talk about it anymore till we get to where we're bound. Shan't be long now."

"Oh, very well, tol lol. Tell me what else has been happening. . . . I been away nearly six months, remember."

"There was a big flood up north in Humberland—lots of folk drownded. And the flood came washing down the coast and did a lot o' damage to towns in Essex and Kent. But London was spared—except the new tunnel under the Thames got flooded out and a lot of wolves drownded."

Both of them fell silent, thinking of Dido's father, whose music had been played at the opening ceremony for the new Thames tunnel, and who, not long after that, had been killed by wolves in Saint James's Park.

"How's Sophie?" Dido asked then, shaking herself briskly.

"Sophie? She's wonderful peart!" A note of fond pride came into Podge's voice.

"Can I go and see her tomorrow?"

"No, dearie, you can't, for she's away visiting cousins in Hanover. But she'll be back in two-three weeks and you can see her then, and you can see little Greena-whizz too—"

"Ohhh!" exclaimed Dido. "Has Sophie been and gone and—?"

"Yes, she has! I'm a dad!"

"But, staying in Hanover? Are we pals with Hanover now, then?"

"Oh, yes, we've signed a big treaty of friendship," Podge said. "It's the folks down south who are giving us trouble now. The Burgundians. But His Reverence'll likely give you the tip on all that."

"*Burgundy,*" said Dido. "Where's that?"

47

"Way down south, past Finisterre and Ushant."

"Well, rabbit me if I can see why His Holy Nibs should want to tell me about Burgundy! Let alone fetching me outa my berth for the pleasure. I was hoping to come along and take a bite of breakfast with your da and your brother Wally after we tied up in the port o' London."

"Well, I daresay you still can," said Podge comfortably. "And welcome! If His Reverence don't give you breakfast, that is. Here we are, now, this is his riverside hidey-hole."

All this time they had been driving through marshy meadows with an occasional patch of scrubby coppice-wood, thorn, alder and willow. Dido guessed that they were still close to the Thames River, for they crossed numerous tidal creeks by narrow wooden bridges. Dawn was still several hours away, but the foggy dark was faintly lighter than it had been an hour ago. Dido could now see ahead of them a little one-story building surrounded by a very neatly trimmed hedge.

As the curricle came to a stop by a picket gate, a dark figure armed with a musket emerged from the shadow of the hedge and sharply demanded a password.

"Pendragon!"

"Pass in, then. But only *one* of ye. His Revrince don't want a whole passel of callers."

"That'll have to be you, then, dearie," said Podge. "But His Reverence won't bite ye."

"No. Now I remember the old guy," said Dido. "I met him once before, when King Dick was being coronated."

She made her way cautiously along a narrow path through a very neat front garden that seemed to be laid out as a miniature landscape with model windmills, streamlets crossed by cockleshell bridges, dwarf trees, tiny thatched houses and toy storks nesting on roofs.

Funny sort o' thing for a grown guy to occupy himself with, thought Dido, who did not particularly admire the garden. Specially seeing as how he's the archbishop of Winchester and Wessex. You'd think he'd have better ways of passing his time.

But then she remembered that the archbishop was known to be a great friend of the king, Richard IV, whose principal hobby was collecting ancient games and playing them with his friends and his wife, Queen Adelaide. But she had died a few years ago. So who does the poor old codger play his games with now? Dido wondered as she tapped at the door.

"Come in," called a gentle voice, and she stepped into a shabby but cozy little room with a rag rug on the brick floor, three wicker armchairs, a kitchen table and a great many shell-framed pictures on the walls. A small coal fire burned in the old-fashioned range, and a kettle hummed on the hob.

The old gentleman, who was seated in one of the armchairs, gave Dido a very sweet smile.

"No need for you to present any credentials, my

child," he said as Dido gave him a respectful bob, "I remember you very well from our pleasant tea party after His Majesty's coronation, when you carried King Richard's train."

"Yes. And I remember Your Reverence," said Dido, relieved that she need not present credentials, for she had not the least notion what they were. "You ate nineteen cucumber sandwiches."

"Aha! And you ate seventeen! I have had a few sandwiches prepared for you, recalling that happy day. To think that was nearly six years ago! How time does fly."

Dido accepted a cucumber sandwich from the plate he offered her, thinking that she would rather have a bowl of hot chowder. But it was kind of the old gager to have them made—she did not think he had made them himself, as they were very neat, cut in tiny squares; whereas he was very untidy, wearing a robe made from a worn gray blanket, canvas slippers and over his shoulders a shabby woollen shawl with a great many holes and dangling ends of wool. The only items that suggested he was an archbishop were his purple silk shirt and a great amethyst ring on his right hand.

He poured hot water into a brown teapot with a ring of blue forget-me-nots round its middle and handed Dido a cup of tea, which in her opinion would have been better if he had waited a few more minutes for the tea to brew.

But she said, "Thank you, Your Worship," and sipped it gratefully enough. It was hot, after all. "Can I help you, mister, in some way?" she presently asked, as the archbishop seemed to have sunk into a kind of daydream.

Or nightdream, thought Dido, listening to the far-off cry of a heron or bittern out there in the dark on the marshes. I wonder that coming and perching out here in this boggy spot don't give the old guy shocking rheumatics. She glanced with some disfavor round the dank little sanctuary.

"You can call me Dr. Whitgift," he replied, rousing up a little. "And, yes, it is hoped very much that you may be able to help me and my colleagues in a most difficult, delicate, anxious affair."

"O' course, Your Honor—Doc Whit," said Dido, more and more puzzled. "Any way I kin be useful, I'll be glad to. But what's the hocus?"

"You are great friends, are you not, with His Grace the duke of Battersea?"

After a moment's puzzlement, Dido said, "Oh, you mean my pal Simon, him as used to lodge with my da in Rose Alley? Sophie's brother?"

"Yes, my child."

"Sure, I know the feller well. Him and me's served each other several good turns."

"Just so. Well. Now." The archbishop suddenly stood up, revealing himself to be a good deal taller and thinner than Dido had remembered. He took several nervous turns about the room, picking shells off the mantelpiece and replacing them, opening the door suddenly and looking out, opening the window likewise and thrusting out his head, as if he feared there might be eavesdroppers outside.

Then he beckoned Dido close to him and whispered, "Have you any notion where the duke of Battersea might *be* at this time?"

"Ain't he in his house? Bakerloo House? Alongside the park?"

"No, my child, he is not there."

"Or he might be at Loose Chippings castle, somewhere up north? He has a deal of property in those parts, I fancy."

"No, a search has been made in those places, without any success."

"Blimey," said Dido, suddenly anxious, "you don't think Simon has been took and scrobbled by some havey-cavey fellers—Hanoverians, maybe? But no," recollecting, "us and the Hanoverians is all cobbers now, ain't we? Would it be that other lot, then? Burgundians, is it?"

"Whisht, child!" The archbishop laid a thin, frail finger on his lips. Then he beckoned her closer and whispered, "It is true that the Burgundians are no friends to our poor dear king. I know that well. Thank Providence, very few people in this world are truly wicked, but I have reason to believe that the duchess of Burgundy is a most evil person. She hates dear King Richard."

"Well—then—"

"And another most evil person, unfriend to our king,"

whispered the archbishop, "another most maliceful, untrustworthy character, Baron Magnus Rudh, a friend of the duchess, has just been released from jail, after vowing to be revenged on all those who put him there."

"Well then," repeated Dido, "can't somebody—as it might be the chief constable—can't he lay that pair by the ears?"

"Ah, but they have done nothing, as yet, to justify such an arrest. So far as we know, that is. . . ."

"But if they are such a danger to the king—or Simon—can't they be warned?"

"But that is just the difficulty, my child. *We have lost the king!*"

Dido gaped at him.

"You've lost—?"

"We have lost the king! We do not know where he has got to—where he can be!"

"Croopus!"

"And that is not the worst of the matter," Dr. Whitgift whispered miserably. "For His Majesty is not at all well. In fact—not to put too fine a point on it—he is at death's door."

"What ails the poor old gager?"

"He is afflicted with a suppurating quinsy—the very same indisposition that carried off his father and his grandfather."

"Is he being looked after by a doctor?"

"We don't *know,*" lamented the archbishop. "But we think—this is our only hope—that the duke of Battersea must be with him. They are firm friends, and as you perhaps know, the duke of Battersea is the next heir to the throne, since the death of Prince David of Wales."

"*Is* he?" said Dido, startled. "No, I didn't know that. *Simon* is? Nor I didn't know Prince Davie had died."

"Yes, that happened a few months ago in the northern city of Holdernesse. He gave his life to save a friend. News of his death, I fear, will have been the final blow to King Richard's declining health—coming after the death of his much-loved Queen Adelaide some time ago. They had not been married very long."

"But—hey—hold on," said Dido. "Prince Davie was seventeen or so, warn't he?"

"Ah, *his* mother had been King Richard's first wife, Princess Edelgarde of Flint. She was drowned crossing the Irish Sea—such an ill-fated family . . ."

His voice faded away.

"So," said Dido, bypassing all these deaths, "so King Richard is missing and also my pal Simon Battersea. No one knows where they're at, that right? How long they been gone?"

"Nobody knows that precisely. The king, of late, has been leading such a reclusive life, because of his health. No public engagements. The only person allowed to look after him was a relation, an old lady he calls Madam, who has been his devoted nurse and taken care of him ever since childhood."

"So he and Simon, and this old gal, have all been missing for no one quite knows how long? Holy Peggotty!

What a mux-up," Dido said. It was plain that she thought but poorly of the people whose job it was to take care of the king. "Ain't there anyplace he might be likely to go? Some hideout, a castle in the mountains or a country cottage—like this one here?"

"Well, there are Osborne, Balmoral, Sandringham, Glamis—but a search has been made; he is not at any of those places. The duke's sister is overseas at present. We had hoped that you, being his friend, might know of some sequestered country residence of his—or a cottage belonging to friends—someplace frequented in childhood, an inn, even—?"

Dido grinned a private grin, remembering what Simon had told her about his childhood. He had run away from an orphanage and lived in a cave in a forest for years, looking after a flock of geese. She did not think it at all likely that he would take the dying king to such a refuge.

"But look, Reverence," she said thoughtfully. "If the poor cove is dying—maybe he wants to die in peace without a lot of fussation. *I* should, if I were him. Can't you just let him alone?"

The archbishop let out a squawk of utter disapproval.

"Dear child—no! A thousand times no! The king of this realm to die all by himself without assistance—without the proper ceremonies, without the consolations of religion, without witnesses, evidence, proof, medical testimony . . . ? Besides, there is the coronet ritual—"

He cut himself short abruptly.

"What's that?" asked Dido. "What is the coronet ritual?"

The archbishop said, rather stiffly, "It is a very private, sacred, royal ritual shared by the dying monarch and his archbishop of Wessex. I can tell you no more than that about it. But I may say that without it, the monarch's passing can hardly be considered legal—or even constitutional. . . ."

"Oh, now I get it," said Dido. "What you want is for me to find the king afore he hops the twig, so you can do this coronet thing with him?"

"Indeed, indeed! For if His Majesty should unfortunately pass away without due process, there might be very considerable doubts and difficulties as to the succession."

"Ah, now I begin to twig your lay. There's no son to inherit. So, what's Simon? How does he come into it?"

"The Bakerloo family are cousins of the Tudor-Stuarts, both equally respectable, well connected and ancient, both being descended in direct parallel lines from Uther Pendragon and so from Constantine the Tyrant."

"Don't sound all that respectable to me," said Dido. "Ain't there any other cousins who might step in?"

"Princess Adelaide—before she married His Majesty—had formerly been married to Baron Magnus Rudh, who traced his descent from Vortigern Aelfred, king of the West Saxons, as well as a very ancient

European family—she had a son by that connection, but what became of him I have not been informed. However, if he is alive, he might consider that he has a claim."

"What was his name?"

"I am not certain that I ever heard it."

"Mind you," said Dido, "if I know Simon—and I *do* know him pretty well, he's as decent a young feller as ever came walking down the pike—I wouldn't reckon on his being all that *willing* to step in and have a crown stuck on his head. Who'd say thank you to have sich a job dumped on them? I ask you? He's an easy, free-acting kind of cove; he likes to paint pictures. I don't see him sitting on a throne and being obligated to marry some princess." Here she grinned to herself. "Who'd want that? I'm dead certain Simon wouldn't. Maybe he spirited old kingy away on purpose so's to wriggle out o' the net. . . ."

"If he did so, he did very, very wrong," said the archbishop severely.

"Well, I wouldn't blame him if he did. Not one bit."

"Just the same, child, can you help us to locate them? Rack your brain, cudgel your memory—some passing allusion, some chance recollection may return to help us."

Dido sat silent, racking and cudgeling as directed. Absently she ate the last cucumber sandwich.

"Ain't there any other cousins?" she asked presently.

"Some Plantagenets, I believe—and some illegitimate

descendants of Henry IX and the duchess of Dee, a young female formerly known as Polly Stone—I believe there is Aelfric of Bernicia—"

"Don't sound too promising."

Dido brooded with her chin on her fists.

Presently she noticed that the archbishop appeared to have fallen into a doze.

She had been on the point of making a suggestion, but now she decided to keep silent. And, thinking over the notion that had struck her, she felt more and more strongly that if the king had suddenly taken a fancy to go into hiding—possibly with Simon for company—he had a right to be left to his own devices. A perfect right! After all, thought Dido, a king oughta get better treatment than common people—not worse. If he's sick and wants peace and quiet, that's what he oughter have. It had suddenly occurred to Dido that the person who might well know King Richard's whereabouts was Mr. Greenaway, the father of Podge, who presided over a huge warehouse near Green Bank in the middle of London's dockland. The king used to go and chat with him, Dido recalled, and drink his apple punch and ask his advice about all sorts of problems. Mr. Greenaway knew Simon too.

What was that that Podge had begun to say—something about painting a picture? I'll not worrit His Reverence with this right now, case it's nought but a wild goose chase, Dido decided. I'll go ask Mr. Greenaway first what he thinks. Podge out there will take me to his da; it can't be far from here. Maybe King Dick has holed out there in the warehouse.

But firstways and foremost, I reckon that poor old Royalty oughta have a say in whether he's hunted out of his hidey hole or left on his lonesome.

That is, supposing the cove is still *alive,* she suddenly thought, a horrid possibility striking her.

Well, I'll ask Mr. Greenaway what he thinks—he's got a lot o' sense—and then I'll get back to His Holy Nibs.

She scribbled a note in a notebook that lay on the kitchen table: WILL BE IN TUTCH—YORS, DIDO and let herself quietly out the door. She wouldn't be sorry, she thought, to get away from the archbishop's dank little hideaway.

The moment she was outside, a thick black sack enveloped her from head to foot, and something that felt heavy as a tombstone slammed her hard on the back of her head. Her knees buckled, her eyes shut and she fell forward into a pit of nothingness.

chapter three

"MY BROTHER WILL pay you," said Jorinda to the driver, jumping out of the hackney coach.

"Beg parding, miss, but I druther have the cash here and now, or your bags stays on the roof."

"Oh, bother! You tiresome man! Wait a moment, then—"

She ran up the moss-grown steps to the big double doors of Fogrum Hall and rapped lustily on them with the handle of her umbrella—for rain was falling steadily—rattled the latch and called, "Open up, within there! It's Mr. Lot's sister—Miss Jorinda—open up, I say!"

After considerable delay the doors were slowly opened and an elderly head thrust out.

"Who's that making such a clamoration at this time o' the evening?"

"It's me, Miss Jorinda! I need money to pay the coachman's fee who brought me here. Can you settle him? Or send for Master Lot."

"Nobody said to me as you was expected, miss."

"Well, I'm here now, so will you please do as I say? My bags are on the coach roof."

Grumbling and reluctant, the porter finally made his slow way down the slippery steps, paid the jarvey and struggled up again with Jorinda's luggage, making several trips and complaining more bitterly each time about the weight of the bags and the lack of consideration shown by people who arrived unexpectedly at an hour when all decent householders were about to lock up and retire for the night. "Lucky the bridge wasn't pulled up yet."

"Where is my brother?"

"Master Lot? He's with His Lordship, o' course."

"My father? Is my father out of prison and here already? Oh, that is capital! I did not think he would be here so soon. Take me to them at once."

"Dunno as 'ow they'll be that happy to see ye—females ain't over and above welcome hereabouts."

"Will you kindly stop boring on and take me to the baron! And you might bring some tea and bread and butter—or tell someone else to. I'm sharp set!"

Mumbling and growling even more, the porter dumped the bags and cat basket in the middle of the hallway and started limping along a dimly lit stone-paved passage without looking to see if Jorinda was following

61

him. But she did so, treading close behind, exasperated at his slow shuffle.

Presently he knocked at a door.

"What is it?" shouted a voice impatiently.

"Beg pardon, me lord—there's a young lady here says she's yer lordship's daughter. Miss Jorinda, she says her name is."

There was a flat, flabbergasted silence from behind the door for a moment or two, then a younger voice called, "Send her away!"

"I will *not* be sent away!" exclaimed Jorinda. "I never heard such rude, hateful rubbish! I am his lordship's daughter. Let me in directly!"

She gave a vigorous poke with her umbrella to the aged porter and another to the door, which swung open, and she marched into the room.

It was a dining room, dimly lit by a number of oil lamps. A low red fire burned in the hearth and the remains of a lavish meal were scattered on a fair-sized table. But Jorinda had eyes only for the two people who sat in armchairs on either side of the fireplace.

She approached the white-haired man.

"Sir! I am your daughter, Jorinda! My mother was Zoe Coldacre, who died at my birth. I have come here to love and cherish you!"

"Oh, for mercy's sake, my good girl! Let us not have any sentimental nonsense of that kind, I beg! I assure you that I could hardly be less interested if you were Queen Cleopatra's daughter."

62

After uttering these words the white-haired man gave her a long, cold, smiling, distasteful appraisal. She observed that his left leg and foot were swathed in bandages and that—for some reason—he held a gold-framed hand mirror at which he glanced now and then.

"But, sir! Papa! Do I not remind you of my mother? Of Zoe Coldacre? I am the living image of her! Everybody says so!"

"I have only the very scantiest recollection of your mother, my good girl. Our connection was extremely brief. Now, will you please go away—*far* away—and never come back? Even supposing that you are my daughter—which I take leave to doubt—what possible use would I have for a daughter? I am already cumbered with a son, which is tiresome enough, but has to be borne." And he threw a glance that was by no means indulgent at the other occupant of the room.

Even Jorinda's extremely self-confident nature was fairly quelled by this unwelcoming reception, though she felt, deep inside her, that given time and favorable circumstances, she could certainly win her father's favor and fondness. In the meantime she was not particularly sorry to find that her brother seemed held in no better esteem. When they were younger, living in royal grace apartments in Saint James's Palace, Lot had often teased and plagued her and made her life miserable. After he had been sent to school and she to Coldacre, they had met only on his brief visits there, and she looked at him now with some curiosity to see how he was turning out.

Not particularly well, she decided. True, he had grown very bulky and tall, but his complexion was pasty. His face was not at all handsome and it wore a smug, self-satisfied expression: Plainly he was delighted at his sister's unfavorable reception. His thick, dust-colored hair stood up all over his head in spikes, and his skin was marked by some red, angry pimples.

Eats too many greasy cakes, decided Jorinda. He always used to.

"Papa, what happened to your leg? Was it something they did to you in prison?"

"Oh, really, you wretched girl, will you please go away and stop pestering me?"

"I know a lot about looking after legs," persisted Jorinda. "Granda was always breaking his, out hunting, and now he has terrible gout. Nurse Mara taught me—"

"That old witch. Is she still alive?"

"Yes, but what did happen to your leg, Papa?"

"A sack full of sixpences fell on it," Lothar informed Jorinda. His voice was decidedly malicious, as if he relished his father's slightly ridiculous mishap. He refilled the wineglass that stood on a table near his elbow and took a gulp.

"Sixpences?"

"From the roof of the Tower. They had been left there for safekeeping, and the idle, good-for-nothing guard, to save carrying it down a few hundred stairs, dropped it over the battlements. It fell on Pa's toe, just as he was leaving. How we did laugh!"

"Were you there, then?" Jorinda was surprised. "When he was released?" It's not like Lot to act the dutiful son, she thought. What did he hope to gain from it? Money, probably.

"O' course I was. And what's more, I brought the sack of sixpences away with us. I love sixpence, pretty little sixpence!" he sang in a loud raucous voice.

"Stop that infernal row this instant!" hissed his father. Their eyes met. Lot abruptly quieted down and took another swig of wine.

"Did they give you leave from school, then?"

"This ain't a school anymore. After I burned old Pentecost's book that he was writing—"

"Hey, wait—who is old Pentecost?"

"The Beak, o' course! So he fired me from the school. Or would have. But just at that time, Pa was due to come out of jug, so Pa bought Fogrum Hall, lock, stock and barrel; old Costpenny got the sack and Foggers Hall belongs to Pa and me now."

Jorinda glanced at Baron Magnus and saw that he was inhaling from a jeweled vinaigrette with an expression that made her shiver slightly; she did not quite know why. There was something cold, folded and withdrawn about his look. Not quite human.

"Why did you burn old Pentecost's book?" she asked her brother.

"Oh, I dunno. Just for a jape."

"Stupid sort of jape."

"Better than what's happened to some of the other

65

folks that the Dad didn't care for." Lot sniggered. "The archbishop, the doctor, the jailer—they've all had their quittance. . . ."

"Will you two pray *leave this room* if you are going to whisper and mutter to each other."

"Sorry, Pa."

"But, Papa dear, is your toe really broke? Or is it sprained? May I not take a quick look at it? For inflammation of the members, an opodeldoc plaster is *sovereign*. When I sprained my ankle hunting, Nurse Mara put one on . . . and the pain went in a twinkling! I promise you!"

"It is not the pain!" ground out the baron. "Do you think I would care about a mere pain?"

"What then?"

At that moment there was a tap on the door, and an exceedingly small, grimy boy entered, laboring under the weight of a heavy tray. This he bore with great difficulty as far as the table, then retreated, after a terrified glance at the baron, and scuttled out the door, leaving it open.

Lothar immediately went over to inspect the tray and picked up a slice of bread and butter from it, which he folded into four and crammed into his mouth.

"Hey!" protested his sister. "That was meant for me." And she quickly poured herself a cup of tea before he could move on to that.

"It ain't so much the toe itself," Lot told Jorinda in an undertone, nodding toward their father. "It's the aftereffects of being clobbered by a sack of silver shekels."

"Why? What is it? What aftereffects?"

"Why, sixpences are silver, don't you see? Lordy, it was funny! The sack bust open and the sixpences was rolling all over the shop. It's like being hit by a silver bullet, don't you see?"

"What has their being *silver* got to do with it?"

"Don't you *know*, you dummy? Silver breaks the power of a you-know-what." Lot let his voice sink even lower so that Jorinda could hardly hear him. "That's why he's in such a wax. Now he finds he can see himself in the glass. Puts him in a real bate."

"Should he not?"

"O' course not! Didn't you know *that*? He's mad because I had the sack fetched here. Something special has to be done with it."

Now Jorinda began to recall various dark hints dropped by Nurse Mara in conversation with her grandfather's housekeeper Mrs. Smidge. Looking about the room, she saw there were half a dozen hand mirrors lying about.

Lothar picked up one of these and handed it to her.

"Can you see yourself in the glass?"

"Why, naturally!" Her round pink face dimpled at her in the mirror; her dark eyes sparkled. How *can* Father not like me, not think I'm pretty? she wondered. She asked Lot, "Should I not be able to?"

"If you were one of *them*, you wouldn't be able to."

"Can you?"

"Ay," he said sourly. "I can. But sometimes the change comes on after age twenty-one—so they say."

67

"So Pa's lost his power. . . . How queer. Does that matter?"

"People won't be so scared of him. A leader has to be able to terrify his followers."

"Who is he going to lead?"

"The Burgundians, o' course."

"What about the duchess of Burgundy? Doesn't she lead them?"

"Oh, she don't count. She's only a female. Pa will soon drop her in the basket."

"I wouldn't be so sure of that. Not long ago she came and talked to us at school. Told us not to let our brothers push us around. She looked like a tree that's been growing for five hundred years. Shouldn't think anybody'd push *her* around. So, what does Pa plan to do?"

"Put me on the throne," said Lot with immense self-satisfaction. He was contemplating himself approvingly in the hand mirror and did not notice the look his sister gave him.

"Why not himself?"

"Wasn't born in this country. That rules him out."

Jorinda wrinkled her brow. "I'm sure there were plenty of kings who weren't. What about William the Conqueror? He was born in Normandy."

"They've changed the rules since then."

"I'd think Pa would soon change them again."

At this moment, with an anguished caterwauling, Jorinda's cat, which had been left in its basket in the hall and had taken all this time to scratch a hole through the basketwork, managed to push open the door and make its indignant way toward its owner.

"Oh, poor pusskin! Was it a starving pussums, then? Here, have a bit of ham."

Jorinda took a fragment of fat from one of the used plates on the table. But, before she could give it to the cat, Baron Magnus, his eyes glittering with rage, hoisted himself from his armchair, took six limping, swooping steps toward the animal and wrung its neck.

"I hate cats. I will not have animals like that creeping and sneaking about this house," he hissed. "Pray remember that! And you, girl, do me the kindness to get out of my sight. And out of this house!"

"*Papa!* How could you? You have killed my poor pussums! And under his cushion I was bringing you a letter from the duchess of Burgundy. I shan't give it to you now." Jorinda's voice trembled with shock and outrage. "I was going to find opodeldoc to put your toe—"

"Be silent, girl! Leave me alone. And don't show yourself before me again."

Sobbing with indignation rather than grief—for she had not been especially fond of the cat, which she kept simply because it was the fashion to keep a pet at school—Jorinda stumbled toward the door.

"You go too, boy. And be sure she leaves this house tomorrow."

"Yes, sir. Yes, sir."

"And take that dead animal out of my sight. You can throw it into the moat to feed the pike."

"Are there really tiger pike in the moat?" Jorinda whispered as they walked slowly along the passage. "That's what my driver told me." Her voice was very subdued.

"Lord, yes! Big as bolsters. Take off your arm in one snap. That's why none of the fellers ever dared run away from school no matter how much old Pennycost beat 'em. It'd have meant swimming the moat, 'cos the bridge is pulled up at night. I reckon you musta got here just afore it was hoisted."

Lot had picked up a lamp as they left the dining chamber, and he now opened a door and led the way into a room that appeared to be a classroom. There were rows of wooden desks and a strong smell of ink and unwashed boys. Lot crossed to a window that was protected by bars, opened it, pushed the dead cat out between the bars and let go of it. Jorinda heard a splash.

Lot burst into song.

"I love little Pussy, her coat is so cold. She's gone to the fishes, she'll never grow old." He broke off to say, "You must never sing or whistle in front of the Dad. He can't stand song or music of any kind."

"It was *horrible* of him to kill my cat," Jorinda said angrily, wiping her eyes.

"Well, what did you expect? He's extra ratty just now, because of his toe, I daresay."

"Has he really bought this house?"

"Bet your boots he has. Because it was Ma's once, and he's glad she's gone."

"Where are all the boys? If it was a school?"

"Most of 'em decamped—the ones who had parents in this country. There's just enough left to act as servants. And don't I just give it to 'em. Ha ha ha! *Walker!*"

"What's that moaning I can hear?"

"The wind, most likely."

"No, it sounds like a man. Crying."

"Oh, well," said her brother easily, "maybe it's one of the brats I had to give a licking to, for not coming quick enough when Pa rang his bell."

"Sounds more like a grown man to me."

"Well, it's none of your blazing business! Forget it. Now we gotta think how to get you away from here or Pa will be real mad. There's a carrier's cart comes by at seven in the morning, brings groceries and stuff. You'd best go with him; he'll take you to Clarion Wells."

Jorinda did not argue. Fogrum Hall was no place for her. She could see that. Even the cheap lodging house in Clarion Wells where she had left Nurse Mara would have been better.

"Where can I sleep tonight?"

"In here. The dormitories—the ones that don't have boys in 'em—are full of rats."

"But there's no bed."

"Put three chairs together," Lot told her impatiently. "I'll leave you the lamp."

He had put it on a desk. By its dim light the spots on his podgy face looked larger and blacker. She certainly did not wish for *his* company overnight, but she hated

71

the thought of passing the night by herself in this cheer-less room.

To postpone the moment of being left alone, she said, "Will Papa really put you on the throne?"

"Certain sure. They just have to find old King Dick—wherever he's lurking—and get Alfred's crown off of him—never mind if his head's in it or not, ha ha ha! The Burgundians are due to land any day now; we'll march on London. Hope the Dad's toe is better by then. It bet-ter be, ha ha! It'll all go easy as a greased slide."

What's in it for me? Jorinda wanted to ask, but did not. Instead she said, "Do you know the duke of Battersea?"

"Simon Bakerloo? That snotty bastard? O' course I know him. A conceited, stuck-up, la-di-da fellow if ever there was one. He'll soon have the rug pulled from under him. The Dad has no use at all for any of that lot."

"Who pays for all this?" Jorinda asked shrewdly. "Burgundians don't come on tick, I bet?"

"Oh, the Dad has plenty of mint sauce from Mid-sylvania. Also he plans to sell off Alfred's crown to some foreign excellency—the seljuk of somewhere; I forget who. It's a curiosity, d'you see—nearly a thousand years old. Someone has offered him a shovelful of dibs for it. All we have to do is find the old gager and take it off him."

"How d'you reckon to do that? Where *is* the king? Nobody seems to know."

"There's one that might."

72

"Who?"

"Used to be a crony of my ma." Lot's voice was loaded with spite. "Used to come calling round, all sorrow and smarm. 'Poor dear Adelaide,' all ducky-wucky and itsy-witsy, Carsluith, he was called in those days, till his dad the earl hopped it. Now he's Lord Herodsfoot."

"Oh, yes, I remember him. He knows about games. Collects rare games for the king."

"Ay. Rare games," said Lothar, giggling. He left the room, singing, "Goodbye, little Pussy, your claws are so sharp. You made a fine snack for the pike and the carp."

Jorinda cried herself to sleep, curled in great discomfort on three chairs.

chapter four

SIR THOMAS COLDACRE, the master of Edge Place, ate, every day, what he called a hunting breakfast. This served as a reminder of earlier times, when he had gone out hunting six days a week. Now Sir Thomas kept a manservant, Gribben, standing behind his chair, whose duty it was to blow on a hunting horn every five minutes. Gribben also tended a brandy-warmer, a large bulbous glass about the size of a football, half filled with cognac, perched in a silver cradle over a lighted candle. At breakfast time this stood by Sir Thomas's plate, ready to pour over the helpings of porridge, eggs, ham, fish curry and buttered toast that followed each other on the daily menu. When the brandy had been poured, it was Gribben's next duty to step forward smartly and set light to it with a burning taper; then Sir Thomas vigorously extinguished its blue blaze with his napkin and bolted down each red-hot course in quick order. If Gribben did not step forward smartly enough, Sir Thomas lashed out at him with a hunting crop, which lay by his plate on the knife side.

"Make haste, make *haste*! Hounds will be throwing off any minute now. Scent oughta be breast-high today, no time to lose."

"Yessir," said Gribben, refilling the brandy-warmer, which he did three times at every breakfast, while Sir Thomas chomped on his flaming kedgeree.

Hounds had not met at Edge Place for a score of years.

"Hand me that second plateful of ham, Gribben; I'm sharp set. There's a chill in the air today; it may be a long run. I'll need extra rations."

"Excuse me, sir, Mrs. Smidge carved that plateful extra thin for Miss Jorinda. We're expecting her sometime today."

And indeed at that moment the sound of hooves and wheels clattering over cobblestones was heard down below.

"That'll be Miss Jorinda now, I reckon," said Gribben.

"May the devil fly away with Miss Jorinda! She ought to be at school. Give me that plate of ham. Mrs. Smidge can carve another plateful, can she not? And why couldn't the gal get here in time for breakfast?"

"It'll be on account of the floods, I daresay. Mortal bad, it's said they are between here and Distance Edge

Junction," said Gribben, passing over the ham and standing ready with his lighted taper. "We're lucky Edge Place stands high on the hillside."

Edge Place was an ancient Saxon homestead, built in the shelter of a horseshoe of woodland halfway up the side of the long, commanding rocky ridge of hill known as Windfall Edge that divided the Combe country from the Wetlands. Like many early Saxon manors, the house stood on stone-built legs over an undercroft, where animals and farm implements were housed, with a great hall and living quarters on the first floor, approached up a flight of stone stairs, and on top of that, a roomy loft, where the servants and children had their sleeping quarters.

Now the sound of quick footsteps coming up the stone stairs could be heard; the door flew open, and Jorinda came running into the great hall, her fur coattails flying.

She tweaked off the heavy woollen wig that Sir Thomas wore at all times, planted a loud smacking kiss upon his bald head, then replaced the wig.

"Sorry to be late for breakfast, Granda! But we met the postman plodding along on his dirty old mule, so I have brought some letters you wouldn't have had till tomorrow. Is there any toast, Gribben? I'm as hungry as a hyena."

"Mrs. Smidge will bring you some in a moment, my lady, and a plate of ham."

"No ham for me," Jorinda said with a shudder. "I'm a

vegetarian. I wouldn't touch meat with a pitchfork, not if you paid me." She flung her fur coat over one of the chairs ranged around the massive dining table.

"Vegetarian?" growled Sir Thomas. "First *I've* heard of it! Stuff and nonsense. Twaddle! Eat what you're served, girl, and don't come these puling, sanctimonious ways in my house!"

"Oh, but, Granda, it's very, very wrong to eat live creatures!"

Mrs. Smidge arrived with a plate of toast in time to hear this. Behind her was Nurse Mara with some of Jorinda's bags, on her way to the upper stair, which led out of the great hall.

"Vegetablarian? What's this new come-over, may I inquire?" muttered Mrs. Smidge to the nurse, who threw up her eyes to heaven.

"Fallen in love again!" she hissed. Mrs. Smidge puffed out her cheeks resignedly.

"Who is it this time then? Not the postman?"

"I'll tell you when I've carried these traps upstairs. Is there a cup of tea? I'm parched!"

Mrs. Smidge nodded and retired to the kitchen, Jorinda calling after her, "Bring me a pot of chocolate, Smidgey, and mind it's really hot and sweet! None of your meagre lukewarm brews!"

Sir Thomas was puffing and growling over the letters Jorinda had handed him.

"Russian boots won't arrive for another three weeks.

Just *why*, tell me that? Why can't those lazy dolts deliver when they said they would? Laggardly brutes—irresponsible vodka-swilling nincompoops!" He tipped a gill of brandy into his coffee and gulped it down.

"Russian boots, Granda? What are they? Who are they for?"

"Clever fella of a Russian invented them—can't be *all* bad, those Rooshians, can they? Electric boots, help you walk twice as quick—just the article for getting up to London, over disputed ground, at the double."

"I should just about think so." Jorinda was greatly impressed. "But do they really work?"

"So old Marty Stokes-Belvoir—British ambassador in Muscovy, old schoolmate of mine—so he says. No modern infantry corps should be without 'em."

"Electric boots," repeated Jorinda, a shade of doubt in her voice. "What exactly *is* electricity, Granda?"

"Just a natural force—knocks trees over in storms—produced by friction," grunted her grandfather. "Find it up there in the sky—two clouds thumpin' together. That's all I know. Rub a lump of amber on a piece of woollen cloth—makes scraps of paper fly about."

"I don't see how that can make you walk faster," argued Jorinda, munching a piece of toast, which she had spread with anchovy paste. "And suppose you are on horseback?"

"Oh, you couldn't *ride*. No, no, that would never do, give your wretched mount a wicked shock. But the boots will be just the article for foot soldiers—get them

78

across country at the devil of a pace. Save issuing them with horses."

Jorinda's eyes sparkled with interest.

"Which side are you on, Granda? The Burgundians'? Or the United Saxons'?"

"Hold your tongue, miss! Walls have ears. And it's none of your business."

"Granda, it's common knowledge in Bath that if the Burgundians get into power, they are going to ban foxhunting."

"*What?*"

"Because hunting makes such a mess of the vineyards."

"Who says so?"

"Everybody. So, which are you — ?"

"Hold your tongue, I said!" Sir Thomas, dangerously purple, opened one of his last two letters and stared at it in furious perplexity. "What the flaming blazes is *this*? Knights Templar of Palestina? 'Chain of heroic love and good luck around the globe. All sanctified by His Reverence the Ninth in Succession to the Throne of the World Soul given on the fourth day of revelation at the New Olympus.' What the *deuce* is all this driveling balderdash, may I ask?"

Jorinda jumped up from her chair and went to read over her grandfather's shoulder.

"Oh, it is one of these chain letters, Granda. I know people at school who have had them. Yes, yes, you see, it says you must send it on within twenty-one days, and if you do that, some tremendous piece of good fortune will come your way."

"Send it on where? Send it to whom?" demanded Sir Thomas.

"Oh, to anybody you choose. Send it to friends"—or to enemies, Jorinda was on the point of adding, but she caught Gribben's eye, gave him a wicked grin and slid her hand over her mouth.

"And if I don't send it on, but drop it in the fire, as such a parcel of trumpery foolishness deserves?" snapped Sir Thomas.

"Let's see, umm . . ." Jorinda studied the page of small, densely packed handwriting with a frown creasing her black brows and, after a moment, said, "Oh, well, some misfortune will happen to you then; it doesn't tell you what."

"So who in the world sent me this piece of rubbish?"

"Goodness only knows, Granda. One of your friends, I daresay—somebody who wishes you well." A glint in Jorinda's eye suggested that there was plenty of choice, but she made no suggestion. "I'll help you reply to it, Granda. It will be no trouble at all. Have you any paper? I'll do the twenty copies they say you have to send on. It will be good practice for me; Miss Gravestone kept saying that my handwriting was not sufficiently ladylike."

"Twenty copies? I'm supposed to make twenty copies of this total rubbish?"

In his outrage at such a suggestion, Sir Thomas nearly drank off the boiling balloon glass of brandy. It was deftly fielded by Gribben, who slid it out of reach and substituted the coffee cup.

"Now, now, sir! Best you take it easy for a minute on the settle, until hounds have met. I'll call you in good time before they draw off; don't you fret your head."

But Sir Thomas was reading his last letter, and its contents caused him to explode into a seething incandescence of rage that made his previous vexation seem no more than a mild murmur.

"What's this, what is this? That pestilent boy—can I never have a day's peace from news about his horrible doings?"

"Oh, dear, Granda, is it about Lot? I'm very sorry if he has done something to upset you. What is it now?"

"That brother of yours—oh, very well, half brother—it's not sufficient that he's been expelled from that school of his, Fogrum Hall, for outrageous behavior and burning the headmaster's book—"

"Burning his book—oh, yes, he did say something—" Jorinda began, then clapped her hand over her mouth.

"Some book the fella, Pentecost, wrote, was writing—ask *me*, headmasters ought to be teaching, not writing books; however, that's neither here nor there—your half brother took and burned it. Not only that, but now, it seems, he's been and gone and *bought* the place, Fogrum Hall, so he can't be turned out. What next?"

"*Bought* it?" Jorinda exclaimed in a tone of slightly overdone astonishment. "How could he buy a whole school?"

"That perditioned father of his—yours—came out of jail, as you may have heard." Jorinda nodded. Her eyes were very bright and she had trouble holding her tongue.

"Well, it seems there is a law—Hogben's Law—prevents prisoners in the Tower from making use of any funds they may have in banks—but that don't apply once they are let out, 'parently. Anyhow, it seems your father, Baron Magnus, seems he has assets, estates, overseas in Midsylvania. Settled a sum on your brother Lothar, bought up Fogrum Hall. And the two of them are living there."

"Well, is not that convenient! Are you not delighted? Now Lot and I have somewhere to live and we need not trouble you anymore," Jorinda suggested innocently.

"I'm still your guardian till you are of age, miss!" he growled. "And a pesky thankless task it is, let me tell you!"

"Oh, Granda!" She twitched his wig aside and planted another kiss on the red-hot brow. "You know that you love us, really."

"Not that diabolical half brother of yours, I don't! I don't love him at all. He's no kin of mine, I thank my stars. The sooner I'm quit of him, the better I'll be pleased. I wish the foul fiend would carry him to Tophet."

"But, Granda, if my papa is now so rich from estates in Midsylvania, have you not considered he might be of some *help* in the Saxon uprising? Or is it the Burgundian?"

"Fiddle-de-dee, girl!"

But just the same, despite her grandfather's snub, Jorinda observed a thoughtful gleam come into his eye.

The kitchen of Edge Place was a modern installation; that is to say, it had been improved by Sir Thomas's wife, Theodora, after their marriage fifty years earlier. The lady came from the ancient Palaeologos family and could trace her forebears clean back to the tenth century, when they were Highnesses of Byzantium. She wished her food to be properly cooked and demanded a high-class Roman cuisine requiring charcoal braziers instead of an open fire in the middle of the kitchen. When she had come to Edge Place, the stable was next door to the kitchen, screened off only by a wooden partition, and sparks frequently set fire to this. Theodora had the kitchen moved upstairs to the living quarters and insisted on a granite sink, cupboards and a table made from a four-legged tree fork with a slab of oak the shape and thickness of a mill wheel jammed between its boughs. There were also wooden stools, for the comfort and respite of the kitchen workers, and on a couple of these, eating oatcakes spread with honey and drinking flagons of mead, were Mrs. Smidge and Nurse Mara.

"Vegetablarian now, is it?" said Mrs. Smidge. "That won't last. Do you mind when she wouldn't eat any food that had wheat in it?"

"Ay, and before that she wouldn't touch honey because she said it was robbing the bees?"

"And the same caper with eggs and hens before that?"

63

"And when she was in love with Dr. Fribble she would only wash in water that had been boiled?"

"That was one of the quickest. Came to a stop when he had to lance a boil on her backside."

"And the dentist? Remember the dentist?"

"Ah. She brushed her teeth five times a day for three weeks."

"With a shredded birch twig."

"What brought this one on, then?"

"She fancied a young fellow on the train. He saved her from a mouse."

At this the two ladies laughed so heartily that they were in danger of spilling their mead. "But where does the vegetablarianism come in?"

"Seems he was one. Offered our good game pie, turned up his nose. Only ate an apple. And then, lord! Didn't he kick up a dust when he saw Old Sir's sheep on their way to Marshport. You'd a thought they were his aunts."

"Fancy! What did he do?"

"Turned them loose."

"The sheep?"

"Ay. Every blessed one. Excepting them that had died already. Went a-capering off with the whole clutch of them following him like—like sheep."

"Well, I'll be bothered!" Mrs. Smidge, the daughter of a shepherd, was flabbergasted at this. "Where did they go?"

"Dear knows. It came on to rain cats and dogs so you couldn't see."

"What did *she* say?"

"Fair dumbstruck, she was. I never see her so took. Went quiet. Quiet as a railing. Didn't say a word all afternoon. All the way to you-know-where."

"What happened there?"

"I wasn't asked in." Both ladies raised their brows.

"This one won't last," foretold Mrs. Smidge. "D'you mind when she was so took with the woodman's boy?"

"Ah. And he wouldn't stop his work to carve her a toy boat." The ladies wagged their heads at the shocking memory.

"Well, I'd best go and put away her things." Nurse Mara drained the last drop of mead. "Is there any company expected? That's the first thing she'll ask — after deciding *not* to stop at you-know-where."

Mrs. Smidge shook her head. "Old Sir's fallen out with Lord Scarswood. Boundary troubles. And he was the only neighbor who'd come near the place after Miss Zoe died. As you know."

Nurse Mara sighed. "Eh, dear. I wonder what'll happen now, with *him* coming out of pokey. And that gashly boy. He and his dad bought up Fogrum Hall. Imagine!"

"They did?"

"They did. Lot said it had been his mum's house; now it was hisn, and he'd turn out all the boys and masters and live as he pleased. That's where she went last night.

Sent me to a lodging house. But she didn't get the welcome she was hoping for. Eh, deary me! She was out of there like a pat of butter on a griddle!"

"You'd never think that boy's mum was Lady A."

"No, you would not. She was a sweet lady."

They shook their heads regretfully.

"How did Lady A ever come to marry His Majesty? When she was married to *him* already and had a boy by him, even?"

"Null and void," said Nurse Mara impressively. "That's what His Reverence the archbishop said her first marriage was. On account of Baron Magnus being a you-know-what. Marriages to such as them don't count. His Nibs said."

"Just the same," Mrs. Smidge said doubtfully, "it seems a queer come-out to me. Even more so with King Dick being king. And he was only prince of Wales then."

"Ah, but a king can do as he likes. And he *did* like Lady Adelaide. His first missus was dead, remember. It was love at first sight with Lady A. And with her too, bless her loving heart. *Her* first marriage had been none of her choosing; it was her pa and ma done that to her. She'd never have got spliced to that monster."

"Was that really why King Jim had him sent to the Tower? To get him out of the road?"

Nurse Mara shook her head vigorously. "Never! King Jim 'ud not stoop to such a mean trick as that. He was a gent through and through. And so is King Dick."

"They say he's mortal sick now." Mrs. Smidge sighed.

"Say what you like. They can send Miss Jorinda to school. They can teach her ladylike ways, but with such a dad, who's to know how that one is going to turn out? Her and that brother both—'tis a terrible unchancy strain. I'd not wish it passed into *my* family."

Nurse Mara nodded. "You'd not believe, even if I told you (which wild horses wouldn't drag it from my lips), the things I heard from my sis about the hard times poor Lady A had with *him*—and her only fifteen years old when her pa and ma married her off to him. Many's the time, my sis told me, she thought the poor lamb would be better off married to a wild wolf. Temper! She never saw aught to equal it. And carryings-on. Like with Miss Zoe. And when in the end Lady A decided to cut and run—oh, my word! When she told him she was leaving . . ."

Mrs. Smidge was big-eyed with curiosity.

"What happened? Did he throw a—one of *those?*"

Nurse Mara wagged her head portentously.

"One was just coming on, so his man told my sis, when His Majesty's officers come to the house and arrested him and took him off to the Tower."

"What happened there?"

"Oh, they had a passel of doctors with herbal drops and inhalers and sufflecators to, like, nip the trouble afore it got too far."

"But now he's come out. . . ."

"Ah. And just as bad as when he went in, so it's said. . . ."

chapter five

SIMON WAS MAKING slow progress, leading his mare through wet woodland. The ground was not completely flooded, but so drenched with rain that Magpie sank up to her fetlocks in the soggy soil at every step, and the little sharp hooves of the sheep cut even deeper; they had followed eagerly where Magpie had led, but their pace was beginning to falter and the light was beginning to fail.

If we can't get there before dark, Simon wondered, what will I ever do with them? There are wolves in these woods—bears too, for all I know—and I'm expected; they will be worrying at Darkwater if I don't turn up soon.

As if in agreement with his thoughts, the sheep, who had been dutifully making their way along the forest path behind him with no sound but the patter of a hun-

dred willing feet, suddenly lifted up their voices in a pro-
longed and plaintive *baaaa*.

Hush, now! Simon admonished them (but in his mind,
not out loud), Keep your worry inside your foolish
heads; we don't want every meat-eater in the forest
alerted to the fact that a hundred Sunday dinners are
trotting through their territory!

And in fact a shout coming from a southward direction suggested that the flock's appeal had been picked up
by somebody. In a few moments the sound of hooves
preceded the arrival of two men, richly dressed and
handsomely mounted.

"Hey there! You—shepherd!" said one of the men.
"Can you tell us how to find a way out of this mortaceous
wilderness?"

Simon's jaw dropped in horror. For here was one of
the people he least wished or expected to see: Sir Angus
McGrind, the marshal of the king's wardrobe and
equerry of state for domestic affairs, a rigid, masterful
Scotsman, quick to interfere in any palace affair that
came his way, detested by the king and always on the
lookout for any business that might increase his own
power and importance. But what disastrous rumor had
brought him in *this* direction?

Mercifully he had not recognized Simon, who blessed
the foresight that had made him put on rough country
clothes for this journey, and a stumble of the mare,
Magpie, which had thrown him into a bog hole and
coated his face with mud.

"Where was you wishful to go, worshipful sirs?" he inquired, putting on a rich Wet-country burr.

"Why, we want to know if there is any mansion or manor in these parts where persons of quality, such as ourselves, might be accommodated."

"Eeh, no, *that* thurr baint, your honor," Simon answered at once with the utmost firmness. "Thurr's nob-but barns and shippens—few enow o' them—'less you count a tuthree chapels."

"Ay, chapels. We came across one of those with a crazy old loon of a chaplain who directed us into a bog. But is there no hall, no country seat, no gentleman's abode?"

"Nay, sirs, not as *I* knows on—not 'less you cater on, norrard an' west'ard, till you spies the rail track, an' that'll take ye, bimeby, to High Edge, where owd Lord Lugworthy has his cassel."

"Oh, deuce take it! How great a distance is that?"

"Mebbe not more'n two hours' ride on your lordships' fine hosses."

"Devil take it!" grumbled Sir Angus again, turning his horse's head in the suggested direction. "And, by the by, where had *you* that well-bred beast, fellow? She is no forest shepherd's nag. Did you come by her honestly?"

"Ah, the mare be turble sick wi' glanders o' the gizzard," Simon explained in a suitably gloomy voice. "I be a-taking of her to Goodyer the horse leech in Forest Wells; I be taking her for Farmer Goadby, who lies mortal sick himself wi' a groovy kidney—'tis told how he caught it from the mare. Fancy that! But Mester Goodyer, he'll have the physic for her, no danger. 'Tis Farmer Goadby who lies on's deathbed, so they do say. I best be on my way, sirs." And he led Magpie forward.

"Oh, well. In that case . . ." Sir Angus quite plainly had had some thought of requisitioning the mare for his own use, but now changed his mind. "Come, Fosby," he said, spurring his own horse, "let us follow the young fellow's directions without loss of time. The day darkens." And, as Sir Fosby Killick, the king's physician, followed him, Simon heard him say, "Have you heard of groovy kidney, Fosby? Is it infectious? Is there a cure for it?"

Simon did not catch Sir Fosby's reply.

Greatly relieved to have got rid of the pain and sent them on a wild-goose chase—which might well land them in one of the forest quagmires (And no harm if it does, thought Simon uncharitably)—he pursued his own course in the opposite direction, and the sheep, refreshed by their short rest, followed him trustfully. The news that the two men had come to this spot from a chapel greatly cheered him; he knew there were three chapels in the middle of the forest: Saint Ardust, Saint Arfish and Saint Arling. They formed a triangle with the angles pointing north, west and east; find one of them and he would know which way to go from there.

And, in fact, not more than fifteen minutes later, by following the hoof tracks of the two men, Simon came to a little, semi-ruinous building, set in a tiny clearing surrounded by a ring of tall holly trees. The sheep were

pleased to avail themselves at once of the supper provided by the short grass in the clearing, and so was
Magpie. Simon peered into the dark doorway of the
chapel and called softly, "Father Sam? Are you there?"

"Hush! Yes, I am here, my boy!" Father Sam, a
plump, rosy-faced little man in a surpassingly ragged
and worn robe and cowl, popped suddenly out of the
darkness.

"Second time I've been interrupted in me prayers," he
said reproachfully. "Saint Arling's Day too! Poor old
fella, he gets little enough heed paid to him as 'tis. Never
mind! Never mind!"

"I am sorry, Father."

"Never fret, me boy, His Grace'll be that glad to see
ye! He's been pining."

"How is he?" Simon asked anxiously.

"Not too hearty." The priest shook his head. "The
sight of ye will brisk him up, let us hope. But—betwixt
you and me—not long for this sad world! And raring to
go! So let us hope you can do whatever he's a mind for
ye to do, and that way set his poor soul at rest. For
there's no question he's pining to follow the Lady
Adelaide into the next world, heaven aid him!"

"Just remind me of the way from here, Father, and I'll
be off at once."

"Go between the two biggest hollies." Father Sam
pointed. "And then keep the blackthorns to the left of ye,
the whitethorns to your right, and turn sharp to the right

when ye come to a great chestnut tree. Then cross the brook, wind through the yew coppice and Darkwater will lie before ye." He chuckled. "Finely I misled two grand gentlemen who were here half an hour ago. Lucky they'll be if they reach Clarion Wells by midnight."

"They certainly will," Simon agreed, remembering his own misdirections. He jumped on Magpie's back. "Thank you, Father, and good night."

"I'll be dropping in on His Grace tomorrow, tell him," said Father Sam. "And thanks to your sheep for trimming my assart grass." He extended a hand in blessing, then returned inside the chapel to his interrupted devotions.

Following the old priest's directions, Simon had no further difficulty in finding his way to Darkwater Farm, an ancient moated building of dark red brick with twisted chimneys that nestled in a hollow in the deepest corner of the forest. The moat was fed from a mere, or tarn, of some size, which Simon and his flock had to skirt round before they reached the entrance to the house. The water of the lake looked black, but that was because the trees crowded so close around it; in fact the water was very pure and clear. Magpie and the sheep were glad to take a drink before they all processed over a drawbridge, under an archway and so into the main courtyard of the house, which was not particularly large, but with its farm buildings set round a square.

A gatekeeper came forward to greet Simon and then

pull up the drawbridge. "Save ye, my lord Duke! His Grace has been asking for ye these three hours gone! But where in the world had ye those sheep?"

"Thanks, Harry. I'll go to His Grace directly," said Simon. "I had to rescue the sheep. May they stay here for tonight?"

"Surely they may. They'll save me the trouble of scything the grass. And when they've done that, young Damon can take them over to Pook's Piece. I'll stable the mare for ye, my lord; you hurry on up to His Grace."

Simon nodded, took some packages from his saddlebags and walked across to the main house entrance. There he was received by a stately old lady in a three-cornered headdress of white buckram and a snowy apron over her black dress, who greeted him by a tap on the cheek with a wooden spoon and said, "Bless you, my boy! My nephew will be happy to see you."

"How is he, ma'am?"

She merely shook her head in reply and motioned Simon up a flight of stairs.

King Richard IV was a slight but muscular man in his late forties, with reddish hair that was beginning to turn white, a long nose, a weather-beaten complexion and very bright gray eyes. His face was pale under the tan, and Simon, who remembered him as a brisk, active, outdoor character, fond of hunting and sport, was sorry to see how frail and languid he now appeared. He was lying on a daybed in a large upstairs parlor and, though he wore his usual tartan kilt and velvet jacket, was wrapped in a woollen coverlet. At sight of Simon he brightened visibly and would have risen from his couch, but the old lady prevented him.

"Nay, nay, Richart, bide where ye lie; the laddie can pull himself up a stool."

Simon greeted him formally, "God save Your Majesty!" going down on one knee and kissing his hand.

"Na, na, ne'er mind the formal pishtushery! Cousin Dick will do just fine!"

"Cousin Dick, then." Simon rose to his feet and found himself a stool. "I am very sorry not to see you better, sir. What can I do for you? Why have you sent for me?"

"Ay, well, ye see how matters are; I'm no' lang for this world. I have my ticket of leave."

"It makes me very sad to hear you say that, Cousin Dick," Simon told him truly. But he believed what the king said. "What can I do for you?" he repeated.

"There's two matters on my mind, laddie."

"Yes, sir. What are they?"

"Maybe three," the king said thoughtfully.

"And they are?"

"First, the portrait. Ye ken, in Saint James's Palace, there are likenesses of a' the kings of England back to the auld conqueror himself. Well, I'd think shame to pop my clogs and no' leave *my* image behind."

"If that is all," said Simon, "I'll be happy to paint Your Grace's portrait. I have brought paints with me as your message instructed, and I'll get to work directly. It will be a pleasure—"

"That's no' all," said the king. "I'd like fine if ye could make it a family portrait."

"*Family,* Cousin Dick?" Simon was bewildered.

"The puir ones that went before," explained King Richard. "My boy Davie, he that ended his days untimely, up in the North country, and his bonny mither, Princess Edelgarde, who was drowned, and then my ither wifie, the Lady Adelaide, who was killt by a jack-o'-lantern falling on her. Could ye pit them all in?"

Simon was a little more doubtful about this.

"The Lady Adelaide I could; I have seen her many times and could easily do a rendering of her face. And Prince David I can remember well enough . . . but his mother I am not so sure about."

"Set yer mind at rest," said the king. "I've a miniature of Edelgarde: I carry it always." And he drew out and passed to Simon a tiny oval portrait, no larger than a watch face. It showed a smiling dark-haired girl.

"Ay, she was a fine lassie," said King Richard fondly. "And there was a gey likeness atwixt her and Davie. Can ye render her from that, Cousin Simon?"

"Oh, surely," said Simon, receiving the miniature. "I'll start at once. I'll make a sketch first, for you to see if you like it, and start the painting tomorrow."

"Ay, do so," said the king. "For there's no time to waste. Maybe a week, no more."

Simon looked at him anxiously. "You said there were three things on your mind?"

"Ay, weel, the portrait is one. Then there's the unchancy matter of His Reverence."

"Dr. Whitgift, you mean, sir? The archbishop of Wessex?"

"Ay, then's the one." The king looked a little embarrassed. "There's a ceremony, ye ken, when a monarch is like to meet his end—eh, ye mind—comes to his final moment. . . ."

"Oh, yes. I have heard something about it; he has to do something with the archbishop." Simon wondered what could be unchancy about that.

"Ay. But," said the king, "we don't want His Reverence carfuffling aboot the hoose like a loose cannon until the final moment comes, du we noo?"

"No, I see that," said Simon. "He's a nice old gentleman, but he'd have precious little to do here. But is there not some farmer who would put him up, or some inn?"

"Dear boy, there's nae farm or village closer than Birk Hill. And that's thirty miles if it is a yard. And anither thing: Folk would get wind of my being in these parts if the auld Reverence was dandering to and fro ilka tuthree days."

"Nobody knows that you are here?"

"Nary a soul!" said the king triumphantly. "Save yerself and Madam, and Father Sam and Tammas Lee, who took the message to ye, and he's silent and trustable as a lockit door."

Simon left that unanswered. He had already decided

not to distress His Majesty by telling him that, after delivering his message, the trustworthy Tammas had fallen, drunk and incapable, between the wheels of two carriages in Westminster Palace yard and received injuries from which he had not recovered. Simon had been informed of the accident and had been at the man's deathbed. Tammas had opened his eyes and gasped, "I didna tell! They made me drunk—I that never touched a drappie in my life, not in all my days—but I didna tell! Say that to His Grace the duke. . . ."

"Don't worry . . . the duke knows."

"They twa camstery callants—tell the duke of Battersea—"

"The duke knows," Simon repeated, but Tammas had already shut his eyes and gone elsewhere.

Now, after a moment's thought, Simon said, "Sire—Cousin Richard—why would Sir Angus McGrind and Sir Fosby Killick be wandering in these parts?"

This news flung King Richard into a great agitation. "Saints save us! Ye saw that ill-visaged pair in these wet woodlands? Ye did not tell them that I was here?"

"Would I be such a fool? They were asking about big houses in the neighborhood; I told them there were none closer than High Edge. They took me for a shepherd and Father Sam had already told them the same tale."

"Ay, Father Sam's as staunch as a stone pillar."

"But why? What would have given them the notion to come seeking you in this direction? For I think that was what they were doing."

"Ill chance it was," said the king. "I mind the occasion well. Once at the Court of Saint James's, we were a' daffing about our latter ends—Sir Angus was there—and I was sic a fule as to say that I would like fine to meet my end in a holding in the Wet country, where I had passed happy hours long ago as a young laddie with my cousins. The cunning knave must have recalled my words."

"Who else was there?"

"I canna recall. It is a hard thing," said the king crossly, "if a puir devil of a king canna find himself a decent, quiet deathbed wi'out a wheen skellums sprattling to be at his bedside when the call comes. 'Tis plain self-advancement brings Sir Angus—much he cares for *my* comfort—and there's ithers wi' darker ploys, Baron Magnus and yon harridan the duchess of Burgundy, fine they'd like to get their mittens on Alfred's torque."

He stopped suddenly, and a troubled, lost look came over his face.

The old lady, who had left the room after admitting Simon, now reappeared with a steaming posset in a silver mug, which she placed on a small table by the king.

"Now, now, Richart, that's enough; that's quite enough!" she scolded him. "The laddie is weary with travel, and hungry too, I'll be bound; and you must not work yourself into a fret, indeed you must not. . . . Drink this posset now and take it easy for a while's while. Let the young man rest and return again when you have rested also. . . ."

She laid hold of Simon's arm with a surprisingly strong hand. He, taking the hint, rose to his feet, saying, "I'll come back in an hour or two, sir, when you have had a nap; and when I come I will have the group portrait roughed out for you."

"Ay, do so," said King Richard contentedly. "I'll be blythe to see what you have accomplished."

Downstairs the old lady—she was known simply as Madam by the aged retainers who took care of the house, but she was in fact Lady Titania Plantagenet, the king's great-aunt, sister of King Henry IX—led Simon into a warm and spacious kitchen, where he was given a welcome meal.

"Will you not take something, ma'am?" Simon inquired as she sat opposite him at the long farmhouse table.

"Nay, my boy, we elder ones need little to keep us going. . . . But tell me about the flock of sheep. Where and how did you come by them?" Simon told the history of the sheep and she nodded.

"I would fancy," she said, after some moments' thought, "that those sheep were intended as food for the Burgundian army."

"Ma'am," said Simon, utterly astonished, "what can you mean?"

"I have it on excellent authority," said Madam, "that the Burgundians are planning an imminent invasion of this island. Their wine crop has failed, it is said, due to colder winters, and moreover, they are being harassed by the Euskara from the south; they have already invaded Normandy, I am told. Everybody seems to be moving north."

"But this is dreadful news, Princess —"

"Oh, do call me Aunt Titania. You are my great-nephew too, I daresay, if you are one of the Batterseas."

Simon was deep in thought. "Does Cousin Richard know of this?"

"No, he does not," said Madam firmly. "And above all things, I would not wish him to know. Let his last days be untroubled ones."

"They are really his last?"

"Yes. Only a few days left. And they are already shadowed by several concerns, which I hope he will divulge to you as you paint his portrait."

"Any way that I can help him, my lady —Aunt Titania —you know that I will be glad —will do my very best —to help make his end a peaceful one. Are you quite *sure* about the Burgundians?"

"I have it from a reliable source that they plan to land at Marshport."

"Marshport. Yes, that was where the sheep were to be sent." Simon was dying to ask who or what was the old lady's reliable source. But there was a steely quality about her that discouraged close approaches, however well intentioned.

"Ma'am —Aunt Titania —His Majesty seemed concerned about Baron Magnus and the duchess of Burgundy."

"Ay, and well he might be. My sources tell me that Baron Magnus, having been released from the Tower, has gone directly to Fogrum Hall, where his misbehaved, ill-conditioned son had been sent as a pupil. As ye may mind."

"Yes, I certainly remember Lothar!" said Simon with emphasis. "When Cousin Richard first married the Lady Adelaide and her young son used to be about the Court of Saint James's, I remember that he was in trouble or making trouble from one day's end to the next. He was a terrible boy."

"He was that! Until the king would have no more of him, and Lady Adelaide converted her own childhood home into a school and had Lothar dispatched there, to the great relief of all at Court. But now the boy has bought up the place with his evil father's money, and I've nae doubt turned the school into a nest of conspirators. I have heard—from my sources—that the duchess of Burgundy plans to go there."

"And that is bad news?"

"She is one of Richard's bitterest enemies. Not only did she once hope to marry him herself—much chance the ill-visaged cateran ever had—but she claims that she herself has a right to the throne by her descent from my brother Henry, which is nothing but bare-faced impudence, for her great-great-great-grandmother, Polly Stone, was naught but a milkmaid and one of Henry's passing fancies— What was I saying?"

"That Fogrum Hall is full of the king's enemies."

"Ay. That it is. And you, my boy, must paint his portrait and rid his mind of its cares and ease him to his latter end before they discover his whereabouts and come rampaging here to cut up his peace."

chapter six

WHEN DIDO BECAME conscious again, she thought at first that she was back in the ship, because everything seemed to be swaying about so. But then, as she began to gather her wits together, she realized that the regular sound she could hear was the clip-clop of horses' hooves.

That's rum, she thought. I'm in a carriage, but how did I get here? It ain't Podge's curricle, for I'd feel the wind a-blowing, and I don't. Whose rig is it, and who stowed me here?

The next thing she discovered, when she tried to put this question to somebody, was that her mouth was stuffed full of cloth, with a bandage tied over it; and when, indignantly, she tried to remove the bandage, she found that her hands were tightly bound with rope. In fact, thought Dido crossly, I've been scrobbled like a simple, green ninny. Now, who can have done that? And where the plague are they taking me?

Since nobody was at hand prepared to give her this information, Dido very sensibly decided that she might as well go back to sleep. It was dark and the carriage blinds were down, so there was nothing to be learned from looking out the windows. But before sleeping she went on a mental quest, rummaging in her memory for any recent event that might have some connection with this abduction.

First I was on the ship coming in to dock in the Port of London. Then I was whistled off the ship by a cove in a boat. Then I was picked up by Podge Greenaway in his curricle and taken to collogue with old Reverence Archbishop Whitgift with his plate of cucumber sandwiches. Aha! Now we're coming to the wishbone! His old Nibs wanted me to tell him—croopus, *that's* it—he was a-telling me that they've lost the king, poor old King Dick—yes—and Simon was missing too, and the king's office coves wanted to ask me if I'd any notion where the pair of them might be. . . .

That's it! The coves who have pinched me likely want to ask the same question! But they sure are barking up the wrong cuppa, for I don't know the answer. So they can put that in their hubble-bubble and smoke it. But, thought Dido, it'd do no harm to lead 'em on a mite, maybe, and let on that maybe I do know, but I ain't telling; that way might give Simon and His Poor Old Majesty a mite of breathing time.

The very last thing that passed through Dido's mind came in the form of a vague dreamy question: Did Simon once tell me something . . . that King Dick had once said to him . . . about a place in a hidden corner of a dark, tangled wood with a lake where a whole bunch of nightingales sang . . . his favorite place? From way back when he was a boy?

Then she was asleep.

The next time Dido woke, it was because she had been roused by a considerable clatteration of horse hooves, whinnies, and a chorus of dogs barking and raucous male voices. The carriage was at a standstill, but started suddenly again with a jerk. Changing horses at a post house, thought Dido, but, blimey, where can we be going? Half across England by the feel; we've been hours on the road. And I ain't half hungry!

No one came to give her any food, however, and the new horses—they must be prime stampers; someone's rich, thought Dido—went rattling on at a breakneck pace for what seemed hour after hour. Despite her bound hands, Dido managed, after dozens of failed attempts, to shove up one of the window blinds and to arrange herself on the seat with her legs tucked under her—thank the mickey they didn't tie my ankles too, she congratulated herself—so that she was able to see out as they bowled along.

However, the view of the landscape outside gave her no clue as to where they were going. London-born, Dido had traveled outside the city very little, apart from a couple of trips to Sussex; the forested, hilly countryside beyond the carriage window might have been France, Greece or Scotland for all she knew. Not a live soul in it for miles, she thought with a shiver; who'd want to live in such a nook-shotten wilderness? Give me Battersea any day!

The thought of Greece or France reminded her of what the old archbishop had said about the Burgundians being about to invade; the duchess of Burgundy was an enemy of the poor old king, he had said, and so was somebody else, Baron Magnus Thing. It don't do to be king, Dido thought. You gets enemies like rats have fleas; no, I wouldn't want that job for all the tea in China.

A change in the horses' pace attracted her notice; she looked out and saw that the carriage was turning off the highway, was passing between two massive stone gate-posts with carved griffins on top of them. The griffins were in shocking repair, with grass and ivy growing out of their jaws; and a great rusted pair of gates dangling between the pillars had not been pushed to, probably, for half a century. Beyond the gates ran a wide avenue between two rows of forest trees, some of which had fallen and lain in their places until they were grown over with brambles. Whoever owns this place is mighty chintzy when it comes to upkeep, thought Dido, glimps-ing a vast mansion ahead; its pale stone front was three times the width of the avenue, but the stone was lichenous and moss-covered, most of the windows were dark and the steps that approached the double front doors were stained and crumbling.

Dusk was falling but she saw a weedy moat under a stone bridge. One or two of the windows on the ground floor showed dim lights in them. At least there's folk in the house, thought Dido, and if they want me to sing for them like a canary, let's hope they'll come across with a bite of summat hot; I'd fancy a meat pie now, or a bowl of that chowder they make so tasty in Nantucket. . . .

The carriage drew up at the foot of the broken steps. The doors opened and two men in dark clothes came out of the house. A few words were exchanged with the driver; then the carriage door was flung wide, and without a word to Dido, the two men grabbed her by the feet and shoulders, swung her up the steps and in at the house door, then carried her like a sack for some considerable distance along a stone-paved passageway.

Dido had passed the last two hours of the journey in mincing and munching the bit of cloth in her mouth and gnawing the bandage that held it in place; now she spat it out and demanded: "Where are you a-taking me? What place is this? And when does I get a bit of prog?"

"You keep a still tongue in your head," said one of the men, and swung her so hard that she bumped painfully against the stone floor. "You tell Their Excellencies what they want to know. Then *perhaps* you'll get summat to eat. Not before!"

The passage here took a sharp turn to the right and the men carried her what seemed like another quarter-mile along it. Then she was pitched through an open door and fell in a heap on a damp brick floor. The door slammed and she heard a key turn in the lock.

"Oh, consarn it!" said Dido angrily. She felt really hard done by.

She had come back to England after a well-earned holiday visit to old friends in Nantucket, anticipating, or at least hoping for, an affectionate greeting from her friends Simon and Sophie Battersea and some sort of welcome from her sisters Penny and Is. She certainly had not expected to be kidnapped, deprived of food for twelve hours and flung into a cold damp prison.

"Pigs!" she muttered. Then, because Dido would never let herself be overborne, even by the most dismally unpromising circumstances, she struggled to her feet and looked about her.

There was nothing much to look at.

It was just not dark indoors. Out the window she could see a huge courtyard, paved with gravel, enclosed by the four wings of the house, which must be as big as a palace. Surprisingly, the yard contained two football pitches, with goals. No one was playing football. Two or three windows had lights in them. Most were dark.

Is this place a prison? Dido wondered. It sure isn't anybody's happy home.

Turning to inspect the small room into which she had been thrown, Dido received a shock. There was very little furniture—a table, a chair, and a box. Under the table something moved. A dog? A cat? A person?

Dido was reluctant to feel under the table with her bound hands; she did not want them bitten as well as bound. Instead she shoved the table, which was quite small, with her hip, to expose whatever was lurking underneath.

A pitiful voice said, "Oh . . . don't hurt me! *Please!*"

Astonished, Dido said, "Who the pize are you? Are you human?"

There was a long silence while the voice reflected. Then it said, "Once I was."

"What do you mean?" Dido demanded. "What is this place?"

"It's a school. Fogrum Hall. Or," the voice said doubtfully, "it *was* a school. I dunno quite what it is now."

"Who runs it?"

The voice seemed doubtful about this too. After another long pause—"It was Dr. Pentecost. But he left after Lot burned his book."

"Lot? Who's that?" The name Lot seemed faintly familiar.

"Lot Rudh. His mum was Queen Adelaide."

"Oh, that feller, I know. But his dad wasn't the king—was he?"

"No. Hush, though! You better not speak about him too loud."

"Why?"

"He owns this place now."

"Lot Rudh does? But he's only a boy. He can't own a school."

"He does. His dad came out of prison and bought it for him."

"His dad?"

"Baron Magnus Rudh. Don't speak so *loud*!" the voice breathed.

"Oh, croopus," said Dido. Again she remembered the archbishop saying, ". . . another most evil person, unfriend to our king . . ."

"How could a person come out of prison and buy a school?"

"He owned a gold mine in Midsylvania. Hush!"

"Blimey."

If the baron owned a gold mine, thought Dido, why was he put in prison? Better not ask about that, perhaps. Instead she said, "What's your name?"

"They call me the Woodlouse."

"Why? Who call you that?"

"Lot started it. Because I curl up in a ball when he hits me."

"He hits you? Why?"

"See, I'm his servant. In the school, big boys had smaller boys for their servants. Lot has me. And when he doesn't like the way I make his toast or polish his boots, he hits me. Very hard sometimes. Once he slammed the door on my fingers. On purpose. Once he burned my face with a red-hot toasting fork. You can see the marks."

"Why didn't you tell the boss? Doc Pentecost?"

"Then I'd only get it worse from Lot. Much worse."

"Why don't you get your dad and mum to take you away?"

"How can I? My dad is the governor of New Galloway. That's south of New Cumbria. A letter takes three months to get there."

"I'd run off," Dido said.

"You can't. The moat is full of tiger pike. And alligators. They'd gnaw you to bones before you could swim to the other side. They pull up the bridge at night. Besides, where'd I run to?"

"Why are you in here now, locked up with me? Did you do something bad? Oh, *do* come out and stand up so's I can see you."

The Woodlouse slowly uncurled himself and stood up. He was very small, much smaller than Dido, dusty and untidy, and his face was somewhat streaked with tears. He might be about twelve, she thought.

He said, "They put me in here to make you understand that you *have* to answer their questions. They can make you. They have all kinds of ways of making you answer. Thumbscrews and other things. A thing called the Boot that breaks the bones in your leg. Awful things. The Iron Duchess. And, of course, if you don't tell them what they want to know, they will do things to me too. Like where he burned me. You can see the marks."

"Yes, I see," said Dido. "What's your real name, Woodlouse?"

"Piers Ivanhoe le Guichet Crackenthorpe."

"Well, Piers, for a start, I can't tell these people what

they want to know, 'cos I don't know it myself. So that puts you and me in a bit of a fix, doesn't it?"

"They'll probably kill us," said the Woodlouse. He sounded almost resigned.

"How many boys are there in this school?"

"Used to be about three hundred. But all those left who could, when Dr. Pentecost quit and Lot and his dad took over. The only ones here now are those with parents overseas. Like me. About forty, I reckon."

"Are they decent coves? Or wrong 'uns?"

"Mixed. You see those fingers on the windowsill?" Dido did see them. She had been wondering what they were—half a dozen of them, small and dusty, about the size of clothes-pegs.

"They belonged to a couple of fellers," said the Woodlouse, shivering, "whose dads wouldn't pay the increased school fee. Lot planned to send the fingers to the parents. But the fellows ran away and jumped from the dormitory windows into the moat."

"What happened?"

"The tiger pike got them. So Lot didn't send the fingers. There'd be no point. He told me to show them to you instead."

"I see," said Dido again.

Footsteps came to the door and stopped outside. The key turned in the lock.

chapter seven

GRIBBEN, THE ELDERLY manservant at Edge Place, had been sent on a pensioned-off hunter to the town of Clarion Wells to post off the chain letter. (Growing bored at the task of making twenty copies, Jorinda had reduced the number to six, which were respectively dispatched to her ex-headmistress, the duchess of Burgundy, the prime minister, the chancellor of the exchequer, the foreign secretary, the minister without portfolio and the archbishop of Wessex, whose envelope lacked a stamp.)

"And get some scarlet satin ribbon while you're in town, Grib," added Jorinda, "and a bag of macaroons from the pastry cook's. Smidgey is no hand at those."

"Ay, m'lady."

"And while you're in town, Gribben, you might keep a lookout for the duke of Battersea."

"Battersea, missie? Duke? What like of person would that be, then?"

"Dark hair. Very handsome. Wears a shabby old gray duffle coat, but you can easily see he's quality. And he may have a hundred sheep with him."

"The ones Old Sir was so mad about?"

"Yes; but Granda's not to know where they've got to. Those sheep were going to be butchered to feed the Burgundian army! Sheep have a right to a say in their own destiny."

"Err," said Gribben. "Old master'll be rate put-about if he don't get paid for 'em."

"Oh, what do I care about that? Sheep are living, individual beings! Animals should not be our slaves!"

"Arr," said Gribben. "And what should I say if I see the gentleman? The dook?"

"First, mind you find out where he's staying. Get his address. Second, tell him—tell him he's very welcome to come and call here."

"Urr. But what'll Old Sir say to that?"

"Never you mind! And don't dillydally all day in the town," said Jorinda, suddenly cross. "You tiresome old man!"

Gribben stuck out his lower lip so far that he could have balanced a walnut on it, mounted his aged horse and rode off. Jorinda went back to her attic bedroom under the roof, where she had cut up various articles of her wardrobe and bedclothes and was pinning together a huge patchwork quilt, its colors mainly red and white, with the Battersea coat of arms and the name Simon Bakerloo across the middle.

"Laws, miss, that's handsome," exclaimed Lucy the chambermaid, called in to sweep the snippets of material that lay ankle-deep all over the floor. "How many patches have ye sewn?"

"Two," said Jorinda. "Would you do some for me, Lucy?"

"Love ye, no, miss, I haven't got the time! Mrs. Smidge'd be after me like a rattlesnake did I stop my work for such a fribble."

"Fribble! It isn't a fribble!"

But Lucy had already left.

Half an hour later she came back, however, to say, "There's a kind of waygoing peddler woman at the back door, missie. Would ye care to see what she has in her pack?"

"Of course I would!"

Jorinda flew down to the undercroft, where the peddler woman had spread out her wares on a sheet draped over a bale of straw. She was a tall bony woman with copious white hair swept back and pinned behind her head under a scarf. Her clothes and skin were wrinkled and brown, her eyes a brilliant gray. She gave Jorinda a cordial reception.

"Now here's a lady as I can tell knows what's what! I'll be bound *you* can tell a hatchet from a herring gull, my dearie. See all these fardels I have — the very best quality you'll find this side of the River Tigris — needles, hair dye, mouse-skin eyebrows, strings, lappets of lace, starch for powdering hair, strips of lead for curlers, hair ribbons, fans, face patches. None but the very best, as you'll see, lady dear."

"What's that?" asked Jorinda, pointing to a bulging stoppered bottle of thick green glass seamed over with silvery scratches. It bore a kind of rainbow bloom. It was corked, sealed over the cork with red wax and had a cloth cap tied on over the wax.

"That? Oh, that is something you'll not be needing for a while's while, my lady love; 'tis only a witch bottle."

"A witch bottle . . . what's that?" At once, Jorinda was filled with curiosity.

"Why, dearie, if you believe some evil person has put a curse on you—or is like to—you make yourself one of these bottles. Or, you pay some person as has the power to make you one."

"What's in it?"

The peddler woman glanced to the right and left and, seeing there was nobody at hand but themselves in the undercroft, whispered, "*Piss!* And hair from where the piss comes from! And an eyelash from that same person, and nine bent brass pins."

"What in the world do you do with it?"

"Bury it under your enemy's house, dearie, and it'll make him sick to death. Or his house will burn down. Or both. But *you* surely don't need such a thing, bless your pretty face! You don't have no enemy, I'll be bound."

"N-no," said Jorinda thoughtfully. "Perhaps not, but

I'll lay my granda could use it. He's forever quarreling with Lord Scarswood. And he—" However, she thought better of what she had been about to say and picked up a peacock-feather fan.

"This is pretty."

"Ah, but ye don't want to go for to buy that, my dearie. Peacockses feathers is terrible misfortunate. That's another kickshaw to give to an *un*friend, not to buy for your own use. Now, this ivory fan, that's more suitable for a young lady such as yourself."

It was also much more expensive. But Jorinda bought it and also a bunch of hair ribbons, a tortoiseshell comb and some beautiful flowered Spitalfields silk.

While paying for these purchases, she asked, casually, "Did you hear of the young duke of Battersea being seen in these parts? A handsome young gentleman riding on a piebald mare? With an owl on his shoulder?"

"A young gent riding a piebald with an owl on his shoulder?"

The peddler looked vague, as if there might possibly be some such recollection in her mind, but if so, it was from a long way in the past. At last she said, "I do seem to mind there was such a person seen, some months back. Maybe 'twas in Clarion Wells. Ay, Clarion Wells it was, and he was heading northward toward Wan Hope Heights."

"No chance he was making for Darkwater and Three Chapels?"

"Nay, lovie, Darkwater burned down, didn't you know? 'Tis all blazed away to cinders, so I did hear. The ghosts have their way at last!"

"Ghosts?"

"Darkwater was allus beset by a tribe of ghosts from crusaders' days, my dearie. Now they will have the place all to their own selves. Was that *all* you wished to buy, then, my lady?"

Jorinda looked long and thoughtfully at the witch bottle but in the end decided against it. For one thing, it cost ten pounds.

"You needn't expect you'll get a princely allowance from me, my girl, now you are back at home!" Sir Thomas had snarled at her only that day at breakfast. "Times are hard, the vines failed, rents are down, takings are dwindling and if you choose to come home before term has ended, that don't help me any, for old Madam Whatsername, your headmistress, won't take a penny off the fee, the skinflint! So you'll have to manage on bread and scrape like the rest of the household."

"Of course, Granda," Jorinda had said meekly, though she noticed that "bread and scrape" for Sir Thomas consisted of his usual four-course breakfast.

"Yes, thank you, that is all," she told the peddler. "But if you should see the duke of Battersea on your travels, you might tell him that he will be very welcome here."

"Ah, now, my lady duck," said the woman, regarding her with brilliant eyes, "don't-ee waste heart's breath on that one; he'd bring ye naught but grief and tantrums. Give me a silver sixpence, do-ee, and I'll cross yer palm and bring ye better news."

"There couldn't be better news," objected Jorinda, but she found a sixpence in her purse and impatiently laid it on her palm, from where the peddler woman swiftly removed it and stowed it away among her brown draperies. "Now then, let's see what fortune has in store for 'ee." She bent her shawled head over Jorinda's hand.

"Shall I be a queen? Or the king's sister?" Jorinda asked eagerly.

"That's what they all ask! That's what they all wish to hear! Every milkmaid and chambermaid."

"I'd have more chance than a milkmaid, I should suppose!" Jorinda grumbled.

"Nay, my pretty, your queens is all in the past, leading back a thousand years to the royal house in Byzantium."

"I know all about them. Granda goes on about them for hours together." Jorinda was impatient. "What lies ahead? That's what I want to know."

"I'll tell ye what, mistress." Suddenly the peddler was serious and emphatic. "There's one lies in yer path as has power to do ye mortal harm, somebody as is close kin to ye. Somebody of the male sex as would not scruple to use ye very ill. Keep yer course away from that one; don't ye touch so much as the hem of his coat! Or ye'll be in danger—and worse than danger of this world—danger of things beyond this world, beyond all we know!"

Her speech was so fierce and vehement that Jorinda

was startled into silence. Biting her lip, she watched the peddler swiftly gather all her wares together and pack them into a canvas sack, sling it over her shoulder and stride away down the grassy hill. "Mind what I say, now!" she called back.

Acting on a sudden impulse, Jorinda ran after her and made another purchase. As she walked back toward the house, there came the sound of a trotting horse in the other direction, and she turned to see old Gribben come out of the woods on his flea-bitten gray.

"Did you find the duke of Battersea?" she called hopefully as he dismounted.

"Nay, that I didn't," he answered grumpily. "And I got yer ribbon, but there was nary a macaroon to be found. Here." And he handed her a small bundle.

"Oh, that's too narrow! That's no use at all."

" 'Twas all they had. Some folks is never satisfied. An' I picked up a bundle of mail for Old Sir, and there's one for you—here."

"For me?" Jorinda was all agog. "Maybe it's from the duke—oh." Her face fell as she saw the writing on the cover. "It's from my brother, Lot. What does *he* have to say, I wonder?"

"Dere Sis," Lot had written, "if you have good Ideez for a king's name, send them." Then there was a series of names, some crossed out—Simbert Lamnel, Warbert Purbeck, Lamkin Simbeck, Purnel Warkin—in careful print. Under these, Lot had written, "Sum O the boyz used to laff at my riting. Now their sory. Ha ha!"

"Wasn't there any talk in town about the duke of Battersea . . . and the sheep?" Jorinda asked Gribben.

He was stabling the mare among the pillars of the undercroft.

"No, there warn't," he growled. "But I bought a couple of newspapers for Old Sir. Simmingly the archbishop of Wessex has bin found a mangled corpus outside his front door. *That* won't worrit Old Sir nor grieve him overmuch, I reckon." And he stomped off up the stairs, leaving Jorinda openmouthed at the foot.

She was about to follow Gribben and put away her purchases when she noticed a post-scriptum on the reverse of Lot's letter.

"Dad sez do U no were king has hid king A's crownet? Thatz the trump card dad sez. If so cum bak an tell him."

Knitting her brow over this, Jorinda went up to her grandfather, who was exploding with rage over a communication he had received in the mail.

"Some smooth-tongued insolent fellow has the gall to send me a bank draft for that missing flock of sheep — calls himself the duke of Battersea! I daresay he's no more the duke than I am the seljuk of Rum. How do I know if this is worth the paper it's written on?" Furiously he waved a slip of paper.

"Bank of Battersea; it looks respectable enough, Granda. How much is it for?"

"Two hundred pounds. That's twice as much as that Burgundian agent fella was offering," snarled Sir Thomas. "That's suspicious in itself!"

Jorinda's cheeks were glowing. "Just as I thought! I knew he'd be true and staunch!"

"What are you gabbling about, girl? Now, here's a bit of news in the paper: Whitgift of Wessex done in by wild beasts, gnawed to death on the Essex marshes—"

"Oh, dear! And I had just sent—"

"Well, I can't say I'll weep millstones over him. I mind when he was a lubberly young curate riding a wrong-footed cob, out with the Sheepwash Hunt, and he headed the fox. Never saw such a sapskull in all my days. Nay, he'll be no loss. They'll have to appoint a new one, though, right smartly, for King Dick's on his deathbed, it's said, and there's that doleful business of King Alfred's mortarboard to be gone through."

"Mortarboard, Granda?"

"Oh, some mumbo jumbo got to be gone through before the next fellow can be sworn in as eligible for the throne."

"If the Burgundians should take over this country, Granda—"

"Never you mind about the Burgundians, miss! I'm sick and tired of the Burgundians! I'd rather take my chance with the other lot. Anyway, politics ain't a fit subject for young females."

"But you *like* the Burgundians, don't you, Granda, because they plan to buy your vineyards and turn them into orchards and hop gardens? They say there's a big field of ice floating down from polar regions. . . ."

"Hold your tongue, gal; I've changed my mind. Plain Saxon's good enough for me."

Changing the subject, Jorinda said, "Granda, I've had a letter from my brother Lothar inviting me to go to Fogrum Hall. It's not a school any longer, you know. Lot has bought it with money our father gave him and he's living there and—and our father is there too. . . ." She hesitated over this but went on hastily, "And they want me to come there; they've changed their—shall I go there, Granda?"

Sir Thomas exploded again. "No, miss, you shall not! What? Go and consort with that precious pair? Riffraff if ever there was! Your scapegrace brother—expelled from every decent school, even Fogrum, where he was only accepted because it had once been his mother's home and she was queen of England—a useless, good-for-nothing hobble-de-hoy if ever there was one. And as for that father of yours, I'm sorry he ever took up with my girl Zoe. An ill day that was for her! A man who is a byword and a nayword all over Europe! They should never have let him out of the Tower; that was the only place for him. No, miss, I shall *not* permit you to go and live with them!"

"I might run away," threatened Jorinda.

But at the back of her mind she heard again the peddler's words: "There's one lies in yer path as has power to do ye a mortal harm . . . somebody of the male sex as would not scruple to use ye very ill . . ."

She ran up to her bedroom and went to stare at herself in a mirror that she had found in the root cellar and hung on her wall. She kept it covered by a shawl in case it was really valuable and she was forbidden to have it. It was oval, framed in large pearly stones the size of walnuts.

Jorinda frowned at her reflection, pursed up her lips, smiled so that dimples appeared in her cheeks and then let out a ferocious growl. She put out her tongue at the mirror image and crossly twitched the shawl back over the glass.

She hid a large box under her bed.

chapter eight

SIMON HESITATED IN the doorway, thinking the king was asleep. But the invalid suddenly raised his head from his pillow and said, "Is it today or tomorrow?"

"It's today, Your Majesty."

"Cousin Dick, Cousin Dick . . ."

"Cousin Dick. I have brought a draft of the family portrait for you to look at . . . if you feel up to it?"

" 'Deed an' I do. Bring it here, laddie, and rest it on the old Madam's chair."

Simon had sketched his draft on a piece of board the king's aunt had found for him—it was probably the top of an old table—which he had scraped and rubbed flat with sandpaper. On this he had drawn a family group: the king between his first and second wives, his son Davie, a boy of about twelve, kneeling on the ground in front of the adults. The people sat in a room with tables and chairs, but behind them stretched a huge open land-scape, mountains, forests and lakes.

The human figures were drawn carefully and in great detail; Simon had taken pains to render the likenesses as close to the originals as he could, and he had tiptoed in once or twice to draw King Richard while he was asleep. The landscape and furnishings were sketchily roughed in.

The king studied it for a long time. Then he dashed away a few tears.

"I like it fine, fine!" he said at length. "Ye have drawn the puir lasses as if they sat there in front of ye. Ay, and young Davie too, 'tis the very spit of him. I wouldna have ye alter onything, not a thing. Except . . . could ye no' make the lasses a mite more leesome? A wee bit o' smile, maybe? They're unco' serious! I'd not wish to gae doon to posteerity betwixt sich a downcast pair!"

Simon promised to see what he could do.

"Let's see now, how lang hae ye been here?" said the king. "A full week, is it?"

"No, only four days, Your Maj—Cousin Richard."

"Ah? It seems longer. Have ye no' heard the nightin-gales sing yet?"

Simon was startled. "Nightingales, sir? Surely it is hardly the season for them? I have heard pheasants in the woods, and owls, cousins of my Thunderbolt," he added, rubbing Thunderbolt's tawny head, which the owl gravely inclined toward him.

"Nay," said the king, "the coverts aroond Darkwater

127

are aye weel-furnished with nightingales; ye'll be hearing them soon enow. Old Madam'll tell ye . . ."

He yawned, and his head drooped. But then he anxiously jerked it up again and opened his gray eyes wide. "We maun find it!" he gasped. "We maun find it and give it to His Reverence afore Saint Lucy's Day!"

"Yes, of course we must, sir," Simon answered soothingly. "But there is plenty of time. Saint Lucy's is Midwinter Day, is it not?"

"Och, aye, so 'tis. 'Lucy who scarce seven hours herself unveils.' Ye'll find it afore then, will ye no', like a good laddie?"

"Certainly I'll find it for you, Cousin Richard," Simon told him. "But what is it? Won't you tell me what it is that you want found?"

But the king's head had fallen forward on his chest and his eyes had closed. Simon, alarmed, was about to call the old lady, but she appeared at that moment with a glass of wine and a crusty piece of bread on a gold platter. The wine was dark green.

"Walnut-leaf wine—'tis all he will take now," she said as she caught Simon's eye fixed on the gold-rimmed glass. "That and the very fresh bread—it must be straight from the oven. They keep him going. Come, Richart, come, my bonny boy, take a sip of wine for your auntie Titania!" The king was with difficulty roused from his somnolent state and persuaded to sip a few drops of wine and mumble a small morsel of bread. Then the old lady beckoned Simon from the room.

"He'll doze off now for some hours," she whispered. " 'Tis the best thing for him. When he is awake, he sometimes frets himself into a fever about Alfred's crown."

"Alfred's crown, ma'am? What is that?"

"Oh, it is one of those nonsensical rituals that men invent for themselves," she grumbled. "Grandfather did it, so Papa did it, so I must do it and my son must *certainly* do it! Such troubles as those bits of foolery lead to! There is an old copper coronet, legend has it that it once belonged to King Alfred, and it has come to be the regular practice that when the king of England is on his deathbed, he must pass the coronet—which Alfred is supposed to have worn round his helmet when he fought the battle of Wedmore—the dying king must hand the coronet over to the archbishop, who then puts it on the head of the heir to the throne."

"Oh, now I understand what Cousin Richard was saying about His Reverence. But is the crown not here?"

"*Most* unfortunately my nephew seems to have forgotten what he last did with it. It is like the Christmas tree decorations," the old lady went on impatiently. "Used only once a year—less frequently than that in this case—put away in some safe corner in between times, and who is to say where that corner may be? My nephew's valet might have known."

"Can we not ask him, ma'am?"

"He died last summer, bitten by an adder—such a pity. Such a useful, knowledgeable man."

"Perhaps the archbishop is keeping the crown?"

"No, that is not at all likely. My nephew is fond of Dr. Whitgift but has no confidence in his good sense. He is one of those saints, you know, who are quite useless when it comes to practical affairs. No, Richart would never have left the crown with him."

"Would it be in Saint James's Palace? His Majesty's official residence?"

"Most unlikely. Richart hates Jim Place—never spends needless time there. No, I am certain the crown would not be in London. It is most likely to be somewhere about this house. . . . But where, is the question."

Lady Titania sighed again, and Simon did too. During the past four days he had thoroughly explored Darkwater Farm, looking for a room that might serve as a studio, and he had discovered that it was the most amazing rabbit warren of Lilliputian medieval chambers, some with doors no more than four feet high, once used by tiny ancestors; there were passages only two feet wide, windows no bigger than dinner plates, narrow twisting stairs and huge black beams thrusting across rooms, or vertical pillars supporting ceilings that were crusted and black with four centuries of smoke. To hunt for King Alfred's crown in this aged dwelling would be like searching for a grain of sugar in an ants' nest.

"Then," said Simon, shifting from this daunting prospect, "His Majesty keeps referring to nightingales. Is that—" He hesitated, then went on firmly, "Is that because his mind is—is distracted by fever? Or are there, in fact, nightingales in the woods around Darkwater, even at this time of year?"

"Have you not read your Chaucer?" inquired Lady Titania rather severely.

"I beg your pardon, ma'am?"

"Geoffrey Chaucer, the poet. His *Book of the Forest,* written when he was king's forester of the Wetlands?"

"My lady, I'm afraid that my education was mostly lacking. A large part of my childhood was spent in a cave, you see, along with some geese."

"Was there no public library at hand?" she demanded.

"No."

"Oh! Well, this poet, Chaucer, wrote some lines about Darkwater in his Forest poem: *'By Darkwater so stille, Oft ye may heare Midwinter Nightingale for human ears tell out her piteous tale.'* Darkwater has always been famous for its nightingales."

"I see. When was Chaucer?"

"Fourteenth century."

"And the nightingales are still here?"

"They do not, of course, perform their full repertoire in winter," acknowledged Lady Titania. "But even so, you may hear them sing from time to time. And there is a well-established local legend that when the king of England lies on his deathbed, all of them will sing all night."

A thoughtful silence fell between them. Then Simon said, "No wonder His Majesty is so concerned. Midwinter Nightingale. That would be on Saint Lucy's Day?"

"Yes."

"I wonder how the story started?"

"Oh, I started it," said Lady Titania. "I have the gift of prophecy. Sometimes I can look at a hand, or a face, and tell what is going to happen to that person in the future. Not always—but sometimes. Would you like me to look at your hand?"

"No, not at all, thank you, ma'am," said Simon firmly. "I don't want to know ahead."

"Very sensible! And just as well, for I'm not sure that I could do it with you. Some are clear; some are not. You have a friend called Dido, I believe?"

"Yes. She is in Nantucket just now."

"No. She has recently returned to this country."

"Oh, I'm very glad to hear that. She might be just the person to find King Alfred's crown."

"Perhaps. Just at present," said Lady Titania, "I have the impression that she is in considerable peril."

"*Dido* is? Where?"

"She is in most disagreeable company. With Zoe Coldacre's malevolent husband and that unpleasant dyslexic boy, her stepson. And that truly evil woman, Minna Mortimer, the duchess of Burgundy. Whenever trouble is brewing, you may be sure that Minna has a hand in it."

"But Dido—?"

"Yes. Your friend Dido," pronounced Lady Titania, "is at this time in grave danger."

chapter nine

DIDO WAS DRAGGED rapidly along the corridor by
two large male persons; she could not see their faces, for
they wore black hoods, but she could tell their sex from
their size and voices.

"Where do we take her?" asked one.

"To the conference chamber," said the other.

Dido wished furiously that while talking to the
Woodlouse she had had the sense to ask him to cut through
the rope that tied her wrists. But perhaps he wouldn't have
had the courage, she thought. Poor little weasel, he seemed
to have had all the spunk drained out of him.

The two men climbed a flight of stairs—this was very
uncomfortable for Dido, since the edges of the stairs
caught her on heels and thighs—and carried her into a
large, well-lit room, where they let go of her so that she
fell on the floor.

"Stand up," said one of the men. When Dido did not do so immediately, he kicked her.

"Do as we say, or you'll get worse than that!"

Angrily, Dido scrambled to her feet. She might have said something that would certainly have led to trouble, but at that moment three people came into the room and climbed onto a platform that was between Dido and the immense window, and she was so startled and interested by their appearance that she held her tongue. A man following the three dumped a heavy canvas sack, which sounded as if it held money, on the floor near the platform. Then he left, shutting the door behind him.

The three people consisted of a spotty boy, a hugely fat woman and a white-haired man.

The boy was known to Dido; she remembered having seen him several times at the court of King Richard. His name was Lothar or Lot. And a horrible pest he was, she recalled. Always playing disgusting jokes and making spiteful remarks. He was Queen Adelaide's boy, because she had been married before, and he was sore because he'd never be king. His dad was in prison for something bad. Ask *me*, thought Dido, King Richard made a rare mistake marrying somebody who had an old husband in jail. He mighta known that would lead to trouble.

The boy Lot was bigger now, and spottier, but otherwise he seemed unchanged. He gave Dido a malicious smirk and said something in a low voice to the fat lady that made her nod with a grim smile.

She'll be the duchess of Burgundy, I reckon, Dido

guessed. She remembered Dr. Whitgift saying, "A most evil person. She hates dear King Richard."

The duchess certainly looked evil. She had a fat pale face and eyes that lacked any expression. They were like two pickled onions, Dido thought, and her mouth was a thin slit, painted bright red, like a line under the wrong answer to a sum. She had a huge white headdress with a central cone from which flapped a muslin veil and two large white wings like elephants' ears. Must be hard to manage in a gale, thought Dido. But I guess she isn't often in a gale.

It was the third member of the trio who made the most impression on Dido. During her travels in America, she had seen rattlesnakes, and this man reminded her of a rattlesnake; he had the same deadly stare.

The three people sat down on red velvet upholstered chairs. Since they sat in silence and did not address her, Dido took the initiative.

"Good evening, folks," she said politely. "I sure would like to know why you took the trouble to fetch me all this way. . . . That really queers me. And I'd not say no to a bite of supper."

The sound of her own voice cheered her a bit. It sounded so sensible.

Since they did not answer, she looked about the room. It was large, lit by gas lamps, and had rows of chairs facing the platform. Maybe it was a classroom. The window, behind the platform, was huge and went right down to the floor. Through it, Dido could see the moat, floodlit by a row of tall gas lamps on the farther shore. The water, Dido noticed, looked dimpled and active, as if it contained a lively fish population. Tiger pike, the Woodlouse had said. And alligators. Dido wondered how large they came.

The walls of the conference room were adorned with stuffed animals' heads and glass cases containing tools and weapons. "They have all kinds of ways of making you answer," the Woodlouse had said. "Awful things." Dido did not care for the look of the implements in the cases. Still less did she fancy the thing like a suit of armor with a hinged front section attached to its forehead; the front part was hoisted up by a rope attached to a pulley in the ceiling. What was *that* for? Dido wondered.

Since the three people on the platform maintained their silence, Dido calmly dragged out a chair from the front row and sat down on it. One of the two hooded men who stood behind Dido moved swiftly forward, but the white-haired man on the platform made a slight negative gesture with his gloved hand. The man stepped back again. Dido said politely, "Excuse me, folks. I had rather a hard day *and* a night of it. You won't take it amiss if I help myself to an apple and pear."

Silence from the platform.

To disconnect herself from their chilly stare, Dido glanced beyond them, through the great pane of glass and across the moat. She noticed that two squirrels were chasing each other in and out of the clumps of reed that grew on the moat bank. Dido was able to see them quite clearly in the bluish light that shone down from the gas lamps; they twirled their tails, bounded in and out of the reeds, sometimes jumped clean over each other. They were plainly having a good time.

Those three in the red chairs don't know what a fine game's going on behind 'em, Dido thought. Their bad luck. She sat back in her own chair, took some steady breaths and tried to imagine that she was still aboard His Majesty's ship *Thrush*, watching the antics of dolphins or flying fish.

But then a bad thing happened.

Swerving to get away from its mate, one of the squirrels bounded to within an inch of the moat's edge. And a man-sized fish exploded from the water, grabbed the squirrel by one leg and vanished below the surface. It happened with such lightning speed that Dido could hardly believe what she had seen. But the squirrel was gone. Its playmate seemed sad and astonished, ran this way and that, hunting for its lost friend, and at last went slowly up the bank and vanished from view in the shadows beyond.

Dido had had an odd experience before the giant pike pounced on its prey.

Watching the squirrel at the water's edge, she saw the action freeze, as if time had come to a stop, as if she were looking at a static picture of two squirrels among some rushes. Then, loud and clear, like a voice telling her a fact from a history tale, words hummed in her ear: *You will never see that squirrel again*. Next moment, the picture moved; the fish shot out of the water, snatched the squirrel and vanished.

Well, the voice was right, Dido reckoned. I shan't see that squirrel ever again. But whose was the voice? How did it *know*?

She was so perplexed by this mystery—wholly different from anything that had ever happened to her before—that, for a moment, she forgot the three people sitting in silence on the platform.

She almost wondered if she could be dreaming. But no, the ropes around her tethered wrists were tight and sore, she ached all over, she was hungry and tired and longed to lie down; No, it ain't a dream, she decided. I wouldn't ever dream a thing so spooky as those three mum-dumb ones up on the stage. Won't they *ever* open their mouths? Are they trying to play some sort of game with me?

Finally the boy spoke.

"Wouldn't you like to know what some of those things in the glass cases are?" he said. He had a teasing, gloating voice. He couldn't wait to tell Dido something that would frighten her. Dido noticed that the two adults made quick gestures of disapproval as if he had diverged from some plan. But they said nothing.

Dido said, "You want to tell me. So go ahead."

"See that thing like a suit of armor? That's called the Iron Duchess. Do you want to know what it's for?"

"Not partikkle," said Dido. "I'd druther know what I've been brought here for."

"See the front section of the Iron Duchess? When that rope is untied, the front part slams down and shuts. Suppose there was a person inside. See those two spikes where the person's eyes would be? See those spikes lower down? How'd you like to be in there when that lid was shut down? Eh? *Eh?*"

Dido considered.

"I'd be too short for it," she concluded. "My head 'ud only come halfway down its chest. Now, *you'd* be just about the right height for it, I reckon."

The boy seemed a trifle disconcerted.

"Well, there's plenty of things here that you *would* be the right size for," he said after a moment's thought. "See that thing? That's called the Boot. Your legs are shut in it, then they hammer in iron wedges to break your knees and your shinbones. You could never walk again. How'd you like to have that done to you?"

"I'd rather have a slice of bread pudding," said Dido. "How come you don't offer your visitors any refreshments?"

The woman on the platform stirred impatiently. "Enough of this foolishment," she said in a flat, heavy voice. "Girl! Answer the questions I shall put to you. Your name is Dido Twite?"

"Certingly, ma'am," said Dido.

"And you are a friend to this duke of Battersea?"

"Simon Bakerloo? Yus. I knows the chap."

"Do you know where he is at present?"

"Haven't a notion. If I'd a been left in London," said

Dido, " 'stead o' being hauled off into the middle of nevermore, I'd ha' been looking for Simon myself. . . . Maybe he went to Hanover. His sister Sophie's there."

"Who has told you this?" said the woman sharply.

"Blest if I remember. . . ." Dido was vague. "Some chap on the ferryboat, I guess."

"Do, do let me try her in the Boot, Aunt Minna!"

"Be quiet, boy! You are no help at all."

"That ain't true!" cried Lot. "I bet I could get her to tell us! You see those axes, girl? You see those wooden blocks? You know what they are for? See those iron screws? Those are for thumbs! You wouldn't be able to crack walnuts at Christmas once you'd had your thumbs squished in one of those." Lot grinned evilly at Dido.

"Hold your tongue, boy," said the white-haired man. His voice was light and weary; something in its tone made Dido shiver. He don't care about anyone or anything, she thought; he'd watch me being sliced into rashers and not blink an eye. But there's summat on his mind. I wonder what? He ain't easy. I can feel it. Those other two are scared of him, though, and he knows it.

"You very likely are not aware of this," said the woman, "but the king is in great danger. He is gravely ill. Baron Magnus has the receipt for a compound, handed down in his family for hundreds of years, which could cure the king's malady. We need to find him and offer this remedy, do you see? Any day now it may be too late."

Oh, yes, and I'll believe that when I see pigs wearing knee boots, thought Dido.

146

She said politely, "But why are you telling me this, ma'am? If you think that *I* know where His Grace is, you're fair and far wide o' the mark. Saint Jim's Palace is where you oughta be asking. Search me if I know why you think I can help you."

The woman said smoothly, "I believe you also know Francis Carsluith, Lord Herodsfoot?"

Dido was startled.

"Why, yes," she said after a moment. "I met the guy two-three years ago. On an island it was, dunnamany miles away from here. Come back on a ship with him. . . . But he's mostly off ferreting about in the back o' beyond, a-searching for games. . . . I reckon he knows more about games than any other feller around."

The woman said, "Lord Herodsfoot's knowledge of games can be of little service to him at present." She clapped her hands together sharply. The two hooded men behind Dido stepped forward. "Open the box!" ordered the woman. The men carried leather pouches attached to their belts. From those they took hammers and chisels.

Dido had vaguely observed that there was a wooden crate on the floor to the side of the stage, but she had paid it no heed, all her attention being concentrated on her three captors. The crate, or chest, was long and narrow; it looked as if it might contain croquet mallets or hockey sticks. Wisps of straw could be seen sticking out from under the lid, which was nailed shut. The two men prized up the lid and dropped it on the floor.

"Look inside, girl," said the fat woman. Dido stood up, walked forward and looked into the box. What she saw nearly made her heart stop beating.

Lord Herodsfoot was inside.

Dido had met him on a Pacific island, had traveled back to England with him on His Majesty's sloop *Thrush* and had grown to know him well. He was in his thirties, a thin, active, intelligent man with fuzzy fair hair. Now she could only just recognize the shriveled, corpselike creature huddled into the chest among a packing of straw, like a dead bird in a nest.

Was he dead? No, there was a faint movement of breath in the concave chest, which was half covered by some filthy rags of shirt. The mouth was half open, the eyes closed. But they opened slowly and looked at Dido. There was no recognition in them.

"What've you *done* to him?" whispered Dido.

"Will I give 'im a prod, ma'am?" said one of the men.

"Wait," ordered the woman.

The boy Lot left his seat on the stage and, with his hands in his pockets, strolled round and stared down at the man in the box. He said, "Once he came and gave a talk to us at school about Inca games. Stupid stuff! Only fit for five-year-olds."

The woman said to Dido, "You see what happens to people who don't help us. We keep them in storage till they mend their ways."

Dido gulped. "How d'you mean, won't help you?"

"He, of all the king's friends, is most likely to know the

location where the wretched man has chosen to secrete himself . . . but no persuasion will exact the information from him. So—"

"Are you going to feed him to the fish, Aunt Minna?" cried Lot with the liveliest interest and enthusiasm.

The fat woman frowned, but gave an order to the two men, who nailed the lid back onto the crate, taking no particular pains over the job. Then they unhooked the rope from the contraption that Lot had referred to as the Iron Duchess. This caused the front section, with the spikes, to fall into place with a loud clang. At the noise, Lot smirked at Dido, who felt an icy prickle of the spine. Supposing a human had been encased inside that metal suit! But what was happening in front of her was far worse.

She said hoarsely, "You *can't*—you can't—" She tugged at her bound hands.

"But we can, my child," said the duchess of Burgundy. "Furthermore, we can do either of these things to you. And many more."

A length of cord was wound loosely round the long wooden crate. The hook dangling from the ceiling pulley was slipped under it.

"Lift!" ordered the duchess. "Lift now and swing it."

She and the white-haired man removed themselves, without haste, from the platform as the crate, with Lord Herodsfoot inside it, began swinging, faster and faster, across the platform toward the great sheet of glass.

"No!" cried Dido. "No, no, stop it, *stop!*"

But they did not stop. With a final tremendous crash of splintering glass, the crate swung clean through the great window; the cord round the crate loosened and flew off. The wooden case fell into the water. Its trajectory caused it to land near the farther bank of the moat. Dido, from where she stood, could see the eager commotion as all the inhabitants of the water hurtled toward the box and its contents.

"It will take them less than a minute to get inside that lid," observed the duchess. She turned to the two men. "See that the window is replaced. At once."

"Yes, my lady." They bowed and left the room.

"Now do you understand, girl?" said the duchess. "I hope you have learned by this example not to temporize with us."

Dido was shaking with shock. She had not the least idea what temporize meant. She said slowly, as if the words were coming into her head one by one, "Well, ma'am, the only place I can suggest is an island on a river in Scotland. It's called the Garple Burn. There's a mighty lot o' nightingales on that island; my pa made up a song about them for His Majesty:

Heck sirs! Just listen to the nightingales sing!
Jug jug! Tereu! Hey ding-a-ding-a-ding!"

"Be quiet, girl," hissed the duchess.

The white-haired man looked as if he was about to faint. He darted a poisonous glance at Dido.

144

The boy Lot took a flask from his pocket and drank a hefty swig from it.

Collecting herself, the duchess asked Dido, "You think the king might be on that island?"

"He was very fond of it, my friend Owen Hughes told me. . . . Used to go fishing . . ."

"Hmnnn. We shall have it inspected."

Two things then happened. The white-haired man said urgently to the duchess, "Margaret, I must set off, *without delay*, on the Black Pilgrimage. To the city of Chorazim."

"Oh, no! *Why?* Why must you?"

Dido shivered. This announcement filled her with cold fright. She had never in her life heard of the city of Chorazim, but she felt certain that it was a bad place.

The white-haired man left the room. At his departure Dido felt a huge sense of relief, but the duchess seemed decidedly put out by his announcement. "That will delay all our plans," she muttered.

Lothar grumbled "It's perishing slow round here. I could do with a B & S. What do you say, Aunt Minna? And what d'you want to do with the gal? Put her in a box like old Whiskers?"

"First we will send to Scotland, to this Garple Burn Island—"

There was an interruption. A bell rang; there was a knock at the door and commotion in the passage outside, and a voice called, "Madam, there's a messenger from Marshport—Captain Zeal—he says it's urgent."

"Oh, very well, let him come in. Why in the world your father must choose just now for his inconvenient pilgrimage I simply cannot fathom."

"Something to do with the crown, perhaps," said Lothar, bored. Then, apparently hit by an idea, he asked Dido, "Say, gal, d'you know about Alfred's crown?"

"Alfred's crown," said Dido slowly. "No. I can't say I do."

But into her mind floated a memory of Dr. Whitgift saying something about the coronet ritual. That'll be what they're after. That'll be it, no question. I'm glad I put them on the wrong track with that Scottish island. Hope they waste days looking for it. . . . But then she had a terrifying thought. Suppose there is such a place? Suppose that's where King Dick really is? That song seemed so real. . . .

Meanwhile a bearded man in a military uniform had come into the room and was engaged in a low-voiced consultation with the duchess. Dido, whose hearing was razor-sharp, picked up a phrase here and a phrase there. ". . . urgently need supplies for the troops when they land . . ."

She tried to listen through Lot's exasperating gabble: "Of course *I* shall be king as soon as the old man kicks it. Maybe before. D'you understand, gal? Before that I'm going to change my name. The fellers used to sneer at Lot Rudh—used to call me Lottie and Rednosed Rudy. What do you think of Simbert Lamnel . . . ?"

"Boots for the troops ordered from the Continent have not yet come to hand . . ."

". . . or Lamkin Simbeck or Purbeck Warkin . . . what do you say to those?"

". . . and the flock of sheep expected by the commissariat department have not arrived yet; they were expected a week ago. . . ."

". . . or Warbert Purnel, which do you think is best?"

"Oh, I should choose Purbeck Lamkin. I reckon the troops 'ud go for that in a big way," Dido answered inattentively.

The duchess was saying, "Yes, yes, no doubt very inconvenient, but *I* am not to be troubled by such minor matters. Have you news from Caledonia, from Bernicia? It is crucially important to keep track of the movements of those northern Saxons."

"You are not listening to a word I say," grumbled Lothar. "I think Simkin Purbeck is best." He gave Dido a vicious poke to call back her attention. "Stupid gal! I say, I say, Aunt Minna, shan't we chuck her in the moat like Curlylocks?"

"No, I have not done with her yet."

The two hooded men had returned with an outsize pane of glass, which they leaned against the wall.

"Find a box for this one," the duchess ordered them, indicating Dido. "Put her back in the shell room, let her eat air for a few days, maybe a week. Then we'll see if she has anything more to say. . . ."

"Can I tickle her up a bit, Aunt Minna?"

"Yes, I suppose so, but don't damage her—not yet." The duchess's voice diminished as she walked away. The last thing Dido heard her say was "Come to the map room."

The two men grabbed Dido by her arms and towed her away along the passage to the room where she had been before. "We'll find a box to fit you," they promised, and left, locking the door. Dido hoped this meant that Lothar could not get in. She did not at all fancy the prospect of being tickled up by him.

In the meantime she decided that the best thing she could do was go back to sleep, as there was evidently no prospect of getting anything to eat.

chapter ten

"WILL THEY COME to meet me?" asked the king.

"Of *course* they will, Your Majesty," Simon assured him.

"Cousin Dick, Cousin Dick."

"Cousin Dick."

Simon had no idea who *they* were. Every day, at about this time, when afternoon was tending toward evening, King Richard grew unaccountably worried and distracted. He would ask, over and over again, if Simon could lend him the rail fare to Back End. Where Back End might be, Simon did not know, nor what the fare was likely to be, but he constantly assured the sick man that there was plenty, plenty of money in the silk sack that lay on the mantel shelf.

"And they will be waiting there to meet me? And they will know me?"

"Certain sure they will, Cousin Dick."

"And those other ones, the group, the ones in black jackets, they won't stop me?"

King Richard showed great anxiety about "the group in black." He would stare fixedly at the far end of his chamber and exclaim that the men in black were walking in procession from one side of the room to the other, that they must have come to seize him and were liable to do so at any moment. Simon had great difficulty in restraining the king at these times; he was frantic to get off his couch and run for his life. Simon knew that if the king were to stand up and take even two or three steps, he was so weak that he would collapse on the floor. If Lady Titania was at hand when the king fell into such a state, she could quiet him down with the remedies she always carried with her: a few drops of columbine juice or a pinch of fennel powder. But Simon was not qualified to administer these, and Lady Titania, having given the king his lunch, often walked out into the woods looking for herbs, tree bark, fungi, nuts and even samples of soil and chips of rock, which she used for medicinal purposes. So, at these times, Simon had to soothe the king as best he could. Generally, after an hour or two in this feverish state, the king would sink into an exhausted slumber as dark fell.

So it was today.

After Simon had reassured the invalid over and over that there was sufficient money in the royal exchequer for his journey fare to Back End, and that friends would be there to see to his comfort when he arrived, the sick man lapsed into his usual sudden slumber.

Simon, worn out from offering fervent promises and reassurances — and occasionally being obliged to restrain the distraught patient — sat himself down wearily and munched a few fragments of crusty bread left over from the noon meal, for which the king had displayed little appetite.

It won't be long now, Simon thought sadly; I must ask Lady Titania if we had not better send for His Grace the archbishop. I suppose she has a messenger ready.

As Simon reached this decision, his eyes were fixed absently on the end of the room; now he was startled to see a silent procession of black figures progress at a stately gliding pace from one side of the chamber to the other and apparently disappear into the wall. They did this for several minutes. It was like watching a funeral cortege of ghostly monks.

Can this house be *haunted*? wondered Simon. But he did not believe in ghosts and had never heard any ghostly legends about Darkwater Farm.

Then it occurred to him that what he was seeing exactly tallied with the king's account of black figures walking across his bedroom. Simon had always assured the sick man that these figures were imaginary, delusions, hallucinations cast up by his fevered brain. And I still believe that, thought Simon, but how comes it that I am having them too?

Am I going crazy? Have I caught Cousin Richard's malady?

Then another solution occurred to him. There was a sour, dry taste on his tongue from having eaten the left-over crusts of bread. A large flagon of water, with glasses, always stood in the king's bedchamber; Simon himself filled it twice daily from the well in the court-yard. He swallowed a long draft of cold, fresh water. When he looked up after drinking, the dark figures were gone, totally. There was nothing to be seen at the end of the room but a haze of gathering dusk.

It was in the bread, Simon thought. *Something in the bread that he eats for his midday meal makes the king see those spooky figures. But Lady Titania bakes that bread. Does she* know *what effect it is having on the king? Is she putting some drug, some medicine into the flour? Is she doing it to poison him?*

A small crumb of the bread remained on the silver platter. Simon put it into his mouth and sucked it slowly. A last black shape made its fluttering way from side to side of the room, rather fast, as if in haste to catch up with the others.

What should I say to Lady Titania? Why has she done this?

Simon began wandering back and forth across the room, absolutely undecided. Lady Titania seemed wise, kindly, wholly devoted to the king and his interests, but what did he really know about her? Where did she come from? Where had she been during most of the king's reign?

I wish there was somebody else I could ask about this, thought Simon.

There came a tap at the door—a soft, hesitant tap. Simon went to the door and opened it, with his finger on his lips, warning that the patient was asleep. Mrs. Wigpie the housekeeper stood outside.

"I'm right sorry to trouble Your Grace," she whispered apologetically, "but Madam's still abroad in the woods, and there's a person come asking if we want our chimneys swept. What should I tell them?"

Simon stepped through the doorway and closed the door behind him. "*Do* we want the chimneys swept?" he asked.

"Well, no, Your Grace, Mr. Dewdney from Low Edge, he mostly does 'em twice a year, in May and November. 'Count he's been so terrible bad with rheumatics, he's a bit late this year. . . ."

"Do the chimneys need sweeping?"

"Not so's you'd lay your head on the block for," Mrs. Wigpie said doubtfully.

"Would this person do a good job?"

"That I couldn't say, sir."

"Humph," said Simon. "Maybe I'd better come and see whoever it is. His Majesty has just gone off to sleep. He's safe to be left for twenty minutes or so."

"Thank you, sir," said Mrs. Wigpie. "I'm sure I don't

know what's keeping Her Ladyship out so late these days. I expect she'll soon be home with her bits of plants and mosses."

Simon crossed the courtyard to the outer entrance, where Harry the gatekeeper was waiting rather irritably to raise the drawbridge as soon as Lady Titania returned. Rather an odd time for a chimney sweep to call, Simon thought.

The aspirant sweep, who had been sitting on a mounting block, now stood up. With a shock of dismay, Simon discovered two things at once. First, the "sweep" was not male but female, dressed in sooty men's breeches and a black velvet cap. And, second, he knew her perfectly well. She was Jorinda Coldacre, the girl he had met on the train.

He would have turned on his heel and gone back across the yard, but she had already recognized him.

"*Simon!*"

"Oh, botheration!" said Simon.

"What a lovely, lovely surprise!"

"What in the world are you doing here dressed up as a chimney sweep?"

"You don't seem very glad to see me." She pouted.

"Why should I be?"

"*Oh!*"

"What are you doing here?" Simon asked again impatiently.

"I just thought it would be fun to go round offering to sweep people's chimneys. Make a change from boring home. And besides—" She stopped in the middle of what she was going to say.

"Well, we don't need our chimneys swept," he snapped, "so you'd better go back to boring home."

"I thought you said you were going to your aunt in London. I wrote to you there."

"I—I had to put off going," he said lamely.

"Who lives here? At Darkwater?"

"My aunt Titania. Listen, will you *please* go home? And forget you ever saw me here?"

"Why? Will you come over to Edge Place?"

"No, I can't do that."

"Why not?"

"I can't leave Darkwater just now."

"Why not?"

"I can't tell you."

"Can't, can't, can't!" She mimicked him angrily. "Well, I can tell you, you may *have* to, soon. If it rains much more, the dam up on Wan Hope Height will give way and then all this part of the forest will be under twenty feet of floodwater. Then you will jolly well have to leave!"

Simon didn't believe her. And he was growing anxious about the king, left alone for so long. He said, "Look, I'm sorry, I can't stay here talking. And I advise you to go home before it is quite dark."

"Oh, my pony knows the way," said Jorinda carelessly. "I'll tell you a funny thing. The other day somebody told me that Darkwater Farm had burned down. Why do you suppose they did that?"

"I have to go. I'm sorry I can't invite you in. My aunt is out."

Jorinda swung herself onto her gray pony, hoisting her chimney rods jauntily over her shoulder; she hoped that she looked like Joan of Arc. Or Boadicea.

"And I'll tell you something about your friend Dido Twite," she called back spitefully.

"My friend—?"

"It's going to be Rat Week for Dido Twite at the place where she's expected. Maybe she's there already. But I very much doubt if you'll be seeing your friend Dido again. . . ." The gray pony cantered off into the shadows.

Simon strode back upstairs with three new sources of worry. Jorinda had somehow found out that he was at Darkwater. Did she guess about the king? And was it true that the dam on Wan Hope Height was about to give way? And where, in heaven's name, was Dido?

Upstairs, in the king's chamber, he had another cause for worry. The king had woken, tried to get off his couch, become entangled in his covers and fallen on the floor. He was trying vainly to haul himself up by the armchair that Lady Titania sat in when she kept him company.

"Oh, my dear, dear sir!"

"Help, help!" gasped the king feebly.

After a long, breathless, undignified period of struggle, Simon had King Richard back on the bed and re-arranged under his rugs. Aunt Titania's silks, scissors, thimble, embroidery hoop, needle book and emery ball were scattered everywhere about the floor. Simon picked them up and restored them to the rush basket in which they were kept. Near the fireplace he found a little vellum manuscript book, sewn together by a thin leather thong, with its title inscribed in ink: *100 New Embroidery Stitches*. He looked inside the cover and saw a list: Tent Stitch, Chevron Stitch, Pekingese Stitch, Roumanian Stitch and so on. A slip of paper escaped from the booklet and fluttered to the floor. More stitches? No.

Simon picked it up and read, in jagged black handwriting:

Barnard Castle, Bernicia

Keep the Old Boy alive as long as you possibly can. I plan to come round by sea and land an army at Marshport within the next few weeks. Early winter here. Where is the archB of W? Keep him at hand.

Your devoted cousin,
Aelfric

chapter eleven

DIDO FOUND HERSELF in the same room she had been shut in before. Was the Woodlouse here too? Yes, he was. He crawled out from under the table, dusty, grimy, tear-streaked as before.

"Look here," said Dido. "First, have you got anything to eat?"

He shook his head. "No. They said they wouldn't allow me any food till you told them the thing they want to know."

"Then we'll both of us have to starve to death," said Dido. "For I don't know it."

She thought of mentioning her red herring story about the river in Scotland, but then thought again. Maybe there were listeners lurking behind holes in the wall to catch any information that might pass between her and the Woodlouse.

"What did you say your name was?"

"Piers Ivanhoe le Guichet Crackenthorpe."

"Well, Piers, the next thing we gotta do is *whisper* . . . in case there's folk got their three-cheers glued to the keyhole."

She rolled her eyes expressively and raised her brows, looking round the room for possible listening points. Piers seemed perplexed for a moment, then nodded intelligently.

"Got such a thing as a shiv on you, a knife?"—indicating her bound wrists. He nodded again and, a little to Dido's surprise, produced a penknife from his pocket and carefully sawed though the constricting cords. In gratitude, Dido vigorously patted his cheek; he flinched and looked startled.

"Thanks, cully!" Dido whispered. "I was starting to think they'd fall off." She rubbed her tingling palms together.

"Now, the next thing is, how do we get out of here?"

"There's no way," he whispered mournfully.

"Fiddle-de-dee! I've got out of worse places than this." She glanced assessingly round the room, went and inspected the view from the window.

"Tiger pike and alligators," Piers reminded her in a whisper. The moat, disturbingly bubbled and pocketed, lay brightly illuminated by gas lamps.

"So, right, the moat's out. Looks like we gotta learn to fly, Piers."

His face fell. Plainly he had hoped that Dido could

work a miracle. She carefully inspected the room and its contents. One table, two chairs, some lengths of cord scattered on the floor where the Woodlouse had dropped them.

Then Dido had another look at the ceiling. There was a trapdoor in it.

Interrogatively, Dido pointed at it. Piers shrugged. The ceiling was well out of their reach. But Dido, without any more communication, began gathering up the bits of rope from the floor, untying the knots in them, then fastening them together to make one length, more than six feet long.

"Does the trapdoor open?" she whispered. "What's up there?"

"I dunno. I never saw it open. Anyway, how could you get up to it?"

"You'll see." Dido lifted one of the chairs onto the table and climbed up on it. The trapdoor was still several feet above her reach. She clambered down and hoisted up the second chair. It would not stand on the seat of the first one; the legs were too wide apart. So Dido turned it upside down, laying the two seats together.

"Give us a hand now, Piers," she whispered.

"How?"

"Stand on the table and help me balance."

Nervously, unwillingly, he did so. Dido scrambled onto the precarious structure of the two chairs, balancing on the rungs of the top chair, and reached up. Now she could touch the trapdoor with her fingers. She gave it a push and it rose slightly.

"Champion! But I need a stick, or a shovel, or a cricket bat."

"What for?"

"To shove it right up, lunkhead!" Then, seeing that the boy looked rather quenched, Dido ended more mildly, "Just look about, Piers, and see if you can't find summat that I could poke the trap with."

"No, I don't see anything," he reported rather hopelessly after a few minutes.

"Ohhh!" Dido let out a deep breath of frustration. Then, gingerly, she descended from the two chairs and cast her eyes round the room.

There was an empty fireplace filled with a pile of cold white ash. In it, Dido's sharp eye detected something that Woodlouse had missed: a pair of rusty fire-tongs half buried in the ashes.

"That'll do us prime, Piers!" she said in triumph. "Just you pass the tongs up to me when I'm atop of the chairs."

"S-s-suppose somebody hears us?" he stuttered.

"Phooey! Why should they?" Dido retorted, hoisting herself up again.

In fact there was every reason why somebody might hear them, for the chairs overbalanced and fell off the table, taking Dido with them. Piers looked toward the door in terror, expecting that somebody, hearing the crash, would come bursting in. But nobody did.

"Guess they're all at dinner," Dido said, rubbing her elbow and repositioning the chairs on the table. "Now, let's try that again, Woodlouse. Nothing grab, nothing get, my aunt Tinty used to say."

She balanced once more on top of the pair of chairs, Piers passed her the tongs and with them she was able to push open the trapdoor.

"My, oh my, there's a thundering great loft up here! Pass us the candle, Piers, so I can have a look round."

"But then I'll be left in the dark."

"You come up too."

Agile as a squirrel, Dido grabbed the two sides of the trap opening, hung for a moment, then swung herself up and through the square hole. "I couldn't do that," quavered Piers.

"I'll dangle the rope, then, and haul you up. Lucky you're only a shrimp."

She pulled the knotted length of rope from her pocket and lowered one end. With unexpected ability Piers grasped it, gripped it with the outer edges of his feet and allowed himself to be pulled up.

"I still don't see how this is going to help us," he muttered rather hopelessly as Dido relit the candle from flint and steel she produced from her pocket. "They'll know where we've gone as soon as they see the open trap. Then they'll come after us. There's no way of getting out of here. We can't fly."

"Well," Dido argued, "it's still better than being nailed in a box and starved. Maybe we'll find summat to eat up here. This is a huge attic, looks like it runs all around the roof, under the tiles. They'll have a job finding us."

The loft stretched away into darkness in both directions.

"Watch where you put your feet, Piers; step on the joists, not between 'em, or you're liable to put a foot through the plaster ceiling."

The tiled roof formed a triangle overhead and was high enough at the point of the angle for them to be able to stand upright. All kinds of odd items had been stored up there in the course of years; occasionally some planks had been laid over the joists to form a floor for storage. There were canvas bags, chests, portmanteaux, saddle-bags, even articles of furniture.

"I wish someone had thought to bring a bundle o' grub up here," said Dido. "I could just fancy a bite of bread and cheese."

"Lot's grandfather used to own this house," said Piers. "Commander Haakon Hardrada. He was a famous explorer. He sailed to the Umbrage Isles. Some of his travel things are stored up here, I believe. There might be food in them."

"Probably the mice had it long ago. No harm in looking, though." Dido began opening boxes and untying strings. Inside a rather nice little walnut desk, she found a leather-bound diary written in elegant copperplate handwriting.

" 'This is the journal of me, Adelaide of Thuringia.'. . . Hey, she was the one who got to be queen, wasn't she? Lot's mum?"

"This was her house when her father died. Lot was born here."

" 'I have discovered, with terror, that my husband is a werewolf. Oh, what a fearful change comes over him at nightfall.' Hey, that's this Baron Magnus who's just gone off on the Black Pilgrimage today, ain't it?"

Piers let out a gasp of fright. "He has gone where?"

"Said he was going on the Black Pilgrimage to the city of Cora-something-or-other. I heard him telling that old duchess just afore the navy chap came in. What is the Black Pilgrimage then, Piers?"

"It is very bad. It gives him the power to do terrible things. Lot talked about it."

"The way the cove is, even now, he ain't my notion of a Sunshine Boy," Dido muttered. "What's a werewolf, anyhow?"

"Somebody who can change into a wolf at night," Piers told her in a very low voice.

"Holy Christmas! You're not bamming? He can really do that? Have you *seen* him do it?"

"No, no, I haven't. Since he came out of the Tower and came here, I have hardly seen him at all. I think he has been ill. It is his foot. And he has been terribly angry. I heard Her Grace the duchess ask him should she send for a doctor, and he was furious. Said what good would a miserable sawbones do him? He said it was all the fault of a sack of sixpences."

"It's rum they'd talk of such things in front of you."

"Oh, they were talking in Latin."

"You speak Latin, Woodlouse?" Dido said in wonder.

"My grandpa, who was a bishop, made me study it since I was four."

"No fooling! But what has a sack o' sixpennies got to do with old Whiskers turning into a wolf at darkfall?"

"Silver is a very strong aid against the powers of dark," Piers told her. "A silver bullet can kill a vampire. I think the sack of sixpences accidentally fell on him at the Tower! Upset his power."

"What a lot you know, Woodlouse."

Dido put the journal back in the desk, which was otherwise empty. "No, hey, here's a secret drawer. Nothing in it, though. No, wait, here's summat in a little leather case. Feels like a penknife. Yes, that's what it is. Knife at one end, scissors at the other. Mighty handy. I'll have a borrow of it if Lady Adelaide don't object." She slipped it into her pocket.

"No prog, though. Let's go on and find what else they stowed up here."

"The candle won't last much longer," Piers said worriedly.

"Then us'll have to see in the dark." Dido was inclined to add, "We could see by the light you give off, you ray of sunshine!" but did not. After all, she thought, the poor worm's got precious little to be cheerful about: family far away in New Galloway, gotta live in this dismal ken, nowhere to run off to.

They explored on for ten minutes or so, turning a couple of corners under the great rectangle of roof.

"Why did Baron Magnus have you collared?" Piers asked.

"He thinks I know where the king is, because the king sees a lot of my friend Simon Bakerloo. But I don't know where they are. The only place they might be, I suppose, is Willoughby Chase."

"Where's that?"

"In the north. That's where Simon comes from. Blimey," said Dido, "what in creation can this be?" What they had come across were two large square objects blocking their way through the attic. The smaller one was made of metal—lead or zinc—the larger of wood.

"This here's a tank," said Dido. "Full o' water, too; that's handy." And she drank thirstily from cupped hands. "Take a drink, Woodlouse; that'll make ye feel better. But what the pink pestilence can this one be? It's like a huge box. The cook's bedroom? It's as big as a small room—only there ain't any door."

"Perhaps round the other side," suggested Piers, and he began to wriggle on his stomach along the narrow triangular gap, which was all that remained between the larger wooden structure and the slope of the tiles.

"It *is* a room!" said Dido when they had worked their way past it. "And look; here's a whole mess o' candle stubs. That's handy. But what the plague is this thing for?"

Piers had discovered a pair of long poles lying across the joists with some tennis rackets and croquet mallets. To Dido's astonishment, he was suddenly filled with hope and enthusiasm.

166

"Stilts! They are stilts!"

"So what's that to sing about?" Dido picked up a croquet mallet. Now, those would be right handy in a set-to,
she thought.

"I used to walk on stilts through the marshes when I
lived on Aelfy's Isle with Mother and Father."

"So? There ain't any marshes here."

"No, but I could walk across the moat."

"Have a bit o' sense, Piers! First off, how do we get
them *down* to the moat? And, if we could do that, I'd
reckon they are too short; the moat's likely too deep."

"No, look," argued Piers, "you can move the foot-
pieces and peg them in at different heights. And I know
the moat is only five or six feet deep. It doesn't need
to be any deeper, on account of the tiger pike and the
alligators."

"Well, maybe that's so," conceded Dido. "But we still
gotta get them down to ground level. And then, there's
only one pair. Who's going?"

"You," said Piers simply. "You've got friends to go to."

"Yes, but, cully, I can't walk on them things. I never
walked on stilts in my livelong. It'd hafta be you."

"Oh."

"And anyway, we're up here and the moat's down
there."

"Oh, but," said Piers, "this box thing is a lift—if we
could find out how to work it." He sounded unexpectedly positive.

"A lift?"

"A hydraulic lift," said Piers, suddenly knowledgeable. "It's worked by a hydraulic ram, from a stream somewhere out in the grounds. When this house was a proper school, there were maids who used to take clean sheets and pails of wash water up to the dormitories, using this lift. That tank is full of water that works the lift."

"If you say so."

"It goes down to the butler's pantry. And there's a window in the pantry that opens onto the moat."

Piers was plainly so carried away by his notion of walking on stilts through the water that he had become oblivious to any difficulties or drawbacks. Walking on stilts was something he could *do*. He dragged the poles inside the lift, where they only just fit, resting cornerways from floor to ceiling. Then he carefully inspected the levers and dials that operated the hydraulic system. There was no door; the lift was a three-sided box.

Dido was much more dubious. Stepping in beside Piers, she eyed the levers with suspicion. "Are you sure, if you pull that thing, that it won't just drop straight to the bottom?"

"No, that would be the cellars. First it stops at the pantry."

"And what am I supposed to do while you go a-paddling across the moat?"

"This part of the house isn't used now. The butler left, so did the footmen," said Piers confidently. "There's lots of empty rooms you could hide in. And all the cellars.

And I'd go to Willoughby Chase and find your friend Simon and come back for you."

To Dido there seemed so many imperfections in this scheme that she hardly knew where to begin arguing. But as she opened her mouth to protest, Piers pulled a large brass lever and—to her astonishment and dismay—the whole cumbrous contraption began moving slowly downward, shuddering and jerking and giving off, as it did so, a series of ear-piercing groans accompanied by a loud continuous grinding shriek.

"Holy halibut!" said Dido. "I reckon no one has used it for a while."

Even Piers looked a little worried. "We'll just have to hope that no one hears," he murmured.

There were enamel discs set in the wall by the brass handle, marked A, P, C and I. "I expect P is for pantry and C for cellar."

"What about I?"

"I dunno. Perhaps it's the ironing room."

"Let's hope it isn't the interrogation room, where they ask the questions."

"Anyway we're only going as far as P," said Piers, with his fingers on the lever.

Dido had half expected the lift to break the aged cables that held it and plummet down the shaft. But this did not happen. It descended slowly—so slowly indeed as to give her a new worry that someone, alerted by the tremendous racket, would come running to the butler's

pantry, and they would find a reception committee waiting for them when they came to a stop.

They watched the wall sliding past—stone, brick,
beams, plaster—then, jolting and shuddering, the lift
came to rest.

"See! What did I tell you?" whispered Piers in triumph. He worked the two stilts, which were about seven
feet long, out of the lift.

The butler's pantry was a small square room, lit by a
gas bracket, with shelves holding dusty glasses and a
large stone sink. The lift occupied one wall. At a right
angle to it was a window looking out onto the moat.
Beyond the window lay dark water, gleaming and rip-
pling under the arc lights. To Dido it looked unbe-
lievably menacing but Piers eyed it with cheerful
confidence. The thought of walking on stilts, something
he knew how to do, had acted like a tonic on his anxious
nature. Now it was Dido who was filled with doubt and
apprehension.

"Honestly, Woodlouse," she whispered, "don't you
think you'd better let me work out some other plan?
That moat gives me the hab-dabs." She thought of the
squirrel. "Suppose you was to slip, or land one o' the
stilts in a pothole?" But Piers had opened the casement
window and negotiated the stilts through it. He sat on
the windowsill, feet outside, holding a stilt in each hand.

"Don't you fret your head! The water only comes up
to the third hole. I'll get across in a couple of shakes.

And then I'll go up north to Willoughby Chase and find your friend Simon."

"He may not be there! And you don't even know the way."

"I'll ask."

He steadied the stilts, leaned forward and stood up on them. After a moment or two he began walking slowly, standing still for a moment after he had planted each pole in its new position. Dido held her breath.

Then—as when she had watched the squirrels playing—she saw time stand still. The small walking figure vanished; she had a prevision of the moat empty and turbulent, the water whirling and splashing up. . . .

"Piers! Come back!"

"So this is where you got to!" said a voice behind her—a familiar voice full of relish and menace. Dido spun round. There stood Lot, grinning all over his spotty face, holding a pistol, which he was carefully aiming at the figure of Piers, now about twelve yards away, doggedly making his way across the water.

Lot was evidently drunk. His face was flushed, his eyeballs were red, his breath reeked of brandy.

"No!" cried Dido sharply. *"Don't!"*

But he did. His finger was on the trigger and he fired. Piers toppled into the water. There was an instant commotion and a wild whirl of splashing.

"That fixed *him*," said Lot with great satisfaction. "Wretched little slug! There won't be much left of him by this time. And now it's *your* turn." He was clumsily re-loading the pistol.

Dido did not wait. With the croquet mallet she knocked the gun from his hand, then sprang back into the lift and pulled the lever.

"Viper! Vixen!" gasped Lot, rubbing his wrist. "Just you wait a moment till I fix you!"

But the lift bore Dido downward into the dark.

chapter twelve

"I HAVE LOST my hearing aid," lamented the king. "And my keys—where are the keys of the palace?"

The first twenty times the king had put forth this question, Simon had offered a truthful answer: "Your Majesty never had a hearing aid. And the keys of Saint James's Palace are back in London in the prime minister's pocket or with the lord chamberlain."

But as rational answers did not satisfy the king any longer, Simon now said, "Look, here are your keys," showing him a bunch borrowed from Harry the aged porter, and, "Here is your hearing aid," displaying a lump of candle wax, warmed at the fire and squeezed into a complicated shape. With this the king would be satisfied for a short time; then he would ask the questions again.

In the past two days the sick man had become

distinctly weaker—more rambling, more confused, less able to do anything for himself. And where in the world was Madam? She had gone off into the woods yesterday afternoon, as was her habit, but she had not come back when the time came to put the king to bed. Simon had had to do that, assisted by Mrs. Wigpie, the elderly housekeeper. Nor had Lady Titania come back at breakfast time.

"It's not a bit like Madam to stop away overnight," fretted the housekeeper. " 'Tis not like her at all! I jest pray she isn't caught in a flood; they say half the country this side of Wan Hope Height is underwater, and the lake level rising all the while. What'll we do if the dam goes, Mester Simon? We divna stay here; the auld hoose'll be flooded up to the second floor. What shall we do with His Grace?"

"We'll have to move him somewhere else. And I believe we should do it today. Is there a cart or a carriage?"

"Nay, Madam took the dogcart and the auld pony. There's only your Magpie and the carry-chair—and all they blessed sheep."

The sheep were another cause of worry. What would become of them if the level of Darkwater Mere suddenly rose by twenty feet? The only bright spot in this anxiety was that the sheep now had such total trust in Simon, they followed him whenever he went out of doors. Which could be a nuisance at times.

"What is the carry-chair?"

Leaving the king in the care of Harry—all the other

old servants seemed to have vanished, frightened away by the threat of a flood—Simon accompanied Mrs. Wigpie to a harness room next to the empty coach-house, where he found an ancient leather sedan chair.

" 'Twas used by Madam's granfer, time he busted his hip out hunting," explained the housekeeper.

The sedan chair had carrying poles front and back and was intended to be borne by two men. But it also had two iron wheels underneath. Simon tested its weight, lifting one of the poles, and wondered if he would be able to pull it along with the king inside it.

"Harry could help ye, happen," suggested Mrs. Wigpie.

Simon dragged the sedan chair out into the main courtyard. Even without a passenger it was fairly cumbrous, for it had a solid wooden framework, and the seat, roof, sides and front flap were made of massively thick leather, probably ox hide. There was a wooden step for the passenger's feet, and a strap to hold him in position. Just as well, Simon thought, considering how frail and shaky the king had become. *All we need is for him to fall on his nose.*

"But where can we take him that's safer than here? Oh, I do wish Aunt Titania were back!" Simon exclaimed, half to himself. But then he recalled that mysterious note discovered in the old lady's work-basket. Who was Cousin Aelfric? Barnard Castle lay far to the north in the principality of Bernicia, which was ruled by Oswin Cantaguzelos. Oswin was no friend of King

Richard, because he sided with the rulers of Elmet and Lindsey, lands that lay immediately north of London and were in constant dispute about boundaries and customs duties. Could Titania's cousin Aelfric be another contender for the English throne? If only the king were in his right mind! If only it were possible to ask him these questions! But in his present state that was not to be thought of; if he was able to understand at all, they would only distress him dreadfully.

"I'm afeered summat bad's overtook poor Madam. 'Tis not like her to stay away so long wi'out leaving word. And 'tis my thought that we should get His Worship away directly. Look at the level of the watter, Mester Simon; 'tis up to the bridge already. In another hour or so, the bridge'll be underwatter."

Mrs. Wigpie was right, Simon saw.

"If only it didn't rain so hard! We must take the chair over to the door so that His Majesty isn't exposed for more than a couple of minutes."

They did this; then the king was wrapped in several quilts with an oiled silk cover over all, and Simon, with Harry's help, carried him downstairs to the courtyard door. This was by no means an easy task. The king had become so thin that he was not very heavy, but the thinness made his joints and skin acutely sensitive, and he whimpered and groaned and exclaimed that the pain was atrocious, they were killing him, where in the world did they think they were taking him? In the rain too!

Were they mad? Where was Aunt Titania? What was going on?

Some of the layers of quilts had to be peeled off, or they would never have been able to pack the patient and his wrappings into the sedan chair.

"Where *are* we taking him?" asked Simon, when His Majesty had been strapped in, and the apron-front buttoned into place, despite the passenger's cries that they were putting him in prison, they must let him out at once, it was a monstrous crime to fasten him up so, in the dark too!

"I reckon we'd best carry him to Father Sam's chapel," Harry said. "That is uphill from Darkwater. 'Twon't be flooded out yet awhile. And Father Sam will surely know the likeliest spot to keep clear of the floods."

"Can you help me to carry him as far as that?"

Harry shrugged. "Never know till you try," he croaked.

"What about you, Mrs. Wigpie? Will you come along with us?"

The old housekeeper shook her head. "I'll stop here, boy, up in the attics. I've carried a dozen lardy cakes up there, and apples and watter for tea. An' I carried your beautiful picture up there and all His Grace's bits and pieces. The attics won't flood. But here's a little bag of needments Madam packed up for him—in case of flooding—with his toothbrush and nightshirt and his hearing aid."

"I thought he didn't use a hearing aid," said Simon, ashamed that he had not thought of these simple necessaries himself.

"No, but Madam said he would soon need to, and that time'll soon be here. . . . And if Madam should come back before the flood, I can tell her where ye've gone. Now make haste! Watter's over the bridge this very minute."

She was right. Old Harry grabbed the two front carrying poles, Simon took up the rear pair and they splashed through an inch of water that was flowing over the timbers of the bridge.

The sedan chair, with the king in it, was very heavy. At first it was almost more than Simon thought he could manage, and he was extremely worried about old Harry.

"Can you do it?" he called.

"Got to, han't I?" Harry called back.

Going in front, Harry chose the way and struck up a footpath that led away from Darkwater Mere. " 'Tis a shorter way to Saint Arling's Chapel, but over high ground. More of a climb, see, but us won't be flooded this way, nor like to meet any unfriends."

Simon had let out the mare, Magpie, on a long leading rein, and the owl, Thunderbolt, perched on her saddle. He had considered harnessing Magpie between the carrying poles, but dismissed the idea. However, to his amusement and Harry's astonishment, they had not gone more than a hundred yards from Darkwater Farm when the flock of sheep came bustling after them. A dozen sheep squeezed together under the sedan. The height of their backs from the ground was just enough to support its floor and the carrying poles. And this made an immense easement to the weight on the human carriers' arms and shoulders.

"Well, by gar!" exclaimed Harry. "In all my born, I never knowed such a thing! They blessed wethers makes a fair heap of difference. Reckon they'll keep His Grace right snug in there, as well!"

In fact it was plain that the warmth from the wool and the trotting animals underneath him had a very soporific effect on the king; for the first ten minutes, a stream of complaints and lamentations had issued from inside the chair, but these soon died away.

"You don't think he's dead inside there?" Simon queried anxiously. Harry peered through the peephole.

"Nay! Sleeping like a dormouse!"

The sheep too were silent; the only sound made by the procession as it snaked along the woodland path was the squelch of a hundred feet, human and animal, on the sodden, rain-soaked forest floor. Simon was worried about the weather. The rain, which had been continuous for three days, was showing a tendency to change its character; the gray, sullen sky now came wandering down in snowflakes.

"How long will it take us to get to Saint Arling's Chapel this way?" he asked Harry.

"Matter o' forty minutes—don't we meet no hindrances."

There were remarkably few hindrances at present, Simon thought, mentally crossing his fingers. The forest seemed strangely empty; there were no rabbits to be seen, no squirrels, no foxes, no deer. Could they all have fled, seeking higher ground? The only wildlife he thought he saw, a couple of times, and that a long way off in the dim distance, were two bulky shadowy creatures, far too large for foxes and the wrong shape for deer—could they possibly be bears? The idea was so unlikely that he did not even mention it to Harry.

But now there came a small interruption to their quiet progress: The owl, Thunderbolt, suddenly and silently took off from Magpie's saddlebow, lifted into the boughs overhead and returned next moment to perch on Simon's shoulder, clutching a white pigeon.

"Well, I'm blessed! What have you brought me now, Thunderboy?"

" 'Pears to me that pigeon be carrying summat a-wrapped round 'is ankle!" called Harry. "Best we stop a minute and you take a look, Mester Simon."

Conveniently the path here twisted between hip-high boulders. Harry and Simon were able to rest the carrying poles on these rocks and take a much-needed rest; and the sheep gratefully strayed away to munch the greenery on the forest floor.

Thunderbolt gently let go his hold on the pigeon, who seemed uninjured but affronted at his sudden capture and shook his disturbed feathers to rights before fluttering away. A small packet had been attached to his leg, wrapped in oiled silk. Simon undid the wrappings and unfolded the paper inside them. He read: "Dear Cousin Titania: Snow and terrible weather up here hinder our troop setting sail at present. Beat you go to F.H., as I told you in my last letter, to see what they are up to. Pray do your best to keep you-know-who alive. Aelfric Bloodarrow."

Oh, dear, thought Simon. Nobody is as simple as they seem. Not that Aunt Titania did seem particularly simple. Where is F.H. and what can she be doing there?

Frowning, he showed the paper to Harry, who said, "Nay, I'm no scholard, Mester Simon. And don't-ee read it out loud to me; trees have ears, I'm thinking. . . . Best we be on our way."

But before they could move on, an arrow sang between the trees and stuck quivering in the path just ahead of the sedan chair. A voice cried, "Halt! Don't move!"

Simon hastily slipped the paper into his pocket, just as a fair-haired man moved out onto the path ahead of them. He was dressed in tattered gray-green clothes that were a cunning match for the autumnal foliage still hanging on the branches. He had an arrow notched in his bow, and looking past him, Simon could see a number of other men, similarly dressed, similarly armed, in among the trees.

"Don't move!" the man warned again. "Our shafts are tipped with devil's claw juice; one of these through ye and you'd turn up your toes afore you could take another step."

"Who are you?" Simon asked quietly. "And by what right are you stopping us?"

"URSA, that's what we are, young mister," said the man.

"URSA, what is URSA? I never heard of it."

"You shall, very soon, young sir! URSA will soon be a power in this land."

"What is it?" asked Simon again. He looked questioningly at Harry, who shook his head.

"United Real Saxon Army!" said the man proudly. "Soon, I tell ye, you'll be hearing more of us. We're a proper match for all those Armoricans and Burgundians."

"But why are you stopping us?"

"We aim to put down the tyrants. We need money."

"We are not tyrants! We are taking a—a sick friend to Father Sam at Saint Arling's Chapel."

"Let's see your sick friend."

With great caution, Simon undid the buttons of the sedan's leather apron front.

The green-clad man peered in and was evidently somewhat taken aback at the sight of the king's pale, sleeping countenance. Plainly he did not recognize it.

"Wha—who—is it dinnertime? Where am I?" quavered the king.

"Don't worry, Cousin Dick, we shall be with Father Sam directly," Simon reassured him.

"I'm thirsty! I have a pain in my toe! A pain in my tooth! I'm hungry!"

"Very soon, *dear* Cousin Dick, we shall be able to take care of all those things. Will you kindly let us pass?" Simon said to the green man. "You can see that our friend is very ill."

Querying looks passed between the green man and his mates in the trees.

"Got any cash on you?" he asked hopefully.

As it happened, Simon had a hundred pounds on him, in paper money, which had been hastily thrust on him by the lord chamberlain when he had been asked to search for the missing king. But he was certainly not going to part with it to these fly-by-night characters.

"I could let you have a couple of pounds," he said cautiously. "But what do you want money for? How do I know you'd make good use of it?"

He noticed Harry give him a warning glance.

"Us'ud take meditation lessons," said the man unexpectedly. "Into meditation in a big way, us Real Saxons be! Oswin there, he can rise right off the ground when he's meditated for half an hour or so. Alwyn can too."

"What do you need meditation for if you're an army?"

"Binds us together like brothers."

"Oh, very well!" said Simon. He pulled two gold sovereigns from his pocket. "Here you are. Now will you allow us to go on our way?"

"Certingly, guvnor," said the man heartily. "And very

much obliged to-ee. *You* be our brother now. Don't-ee go below this height, mind, in the woods, for the dam's due to bust anytime—there she goes, hark!" he added, as a distant dead sound, between a throb and a thump, quivered through the forest. "Now the water'll come up in a hurry, and bad luck to all the roe deer and foxes that haven't shifted their quarters already. . . ."

"Talking of animals," said Simon, "you live in the woods; have you seen any beasts that look like bears lately?"

The green man grinned. "The bears was the Burgundians' big mistake," he explained. "Ordered 'em from Muscovy, they did, and a pretty penny they Rooshians asked for 'em, so I'm told—and they all took sick, no use to anybody, so they turned 'em loose in the woods. *Boots* was what they had ordered, but bless your soul, they Rooshians don't understand a word of Burgundian, simmingly, and *bears* was what they got. Thank you, young mister, a safe journey to ye."

He and his comrades melted away among the trees. Then, suddenly, he was back again. "They sheep, gaffer? They be yourn?"

"Why, yes," Simon said. "I bought them—paid for them. Why?"

"If ye didn't want them, we could find a use for 'em."

"I do want them."

"No matter." He was gone again.

Simon and Harry picked up the carrying poles. The sheep reassembled themselves under the chair.

"When, when shall we get there?" fretted the king.

"Very, very soon now, Cousin Dick. I can see the spire of Saint Arling's Chapel ahead, past those holly trees."

As they struggled on—both Simon and Harry exhausted by this time, and even the sheep seemed tired—Simon suddenly said, "I wonder what was the matter with the bears?"

chapter thirteen

WHEN DIDO STEPPED out of the lift at the cellar level, she had the presence of mind to scoop up a handful of half-burned candles that lay on the floor before venturing out. She knew that she must waste no time in removing herself, for Lot would surely come down after her as soon as the lift returned to ground level.

It was pitch dark down there. She lit one of her candle stubs, packing the rest into her pocket. Beyond the lift entrance, facing her, she could see a warren of narrow, brick-built vaulted passages that led away in half a dozen directions. Impossible to know which to choose, but the choice must be made fast, for she heard the lift creak and groan as it started on its upward journey.

She took the passage on the extreme left and started along it, noticing that its walls were lined with wooden wine racks containing hundreds of bottles. Wow! Lot must enjoy himself down here, she thought. I bet he often comes down here. Maybe I shoulda taken one o' the other passages, but maybe they are all the same, stuffed with wine bottles.

Before she had gone very far, she almost tripped over a bulky object that lay on the floor of the passage. The object seemed to be a canvas sack containing coins. Realizing that she was almost on the point of collapse, weak and trembling, Dido sat down on it. It chinked. A sack of sixpences, she thought. Who was saying summat about a sack of sixpences? And then she remembered that it was the Woodlouse. . . . Something about Baron Magnus having lost his power because a sack of sixpences fell on him . . . But, if so, why would he keep it in the cellar? You'd think he'd want to get rid of it! But maybe somebody else put it in the cellar?

I must sit still for a moment, thought Dido; my legs feel about to buckle.

In the past couple of hours she had seen two people whom she liked and respected ejected from life as horribly and heartlessly as if they had been wasps or rats. That Piers, she thought, was a real spunky little character, in spite of being scared to death most of the time — and for good reason: He chose to help me and *did* help me, and he was game as a little cock-sparrer when it come to crossing the moat on stilts. Though, mind you, that was a clung-headed thing to do and I only wish I'd stopped him. But he would go. . . .

And, as to what they had done to Frankie

Herodsfoot—it didn't bear thinking about. But she couldn't help the thoughts; they would push in. Dido had encountered Lord Herodsfoot some years ago. They had met on a Pacific island where he was searching for unusual games to entertain the former king, King Richard's father, and Dido was on a roundabout way home to England from New Cumbria. And a right decent cove he was, Dido remembered, a bit vague and wandering in his ways but just as sound as a nut when you got to know him. Why did they ever have to keep him in a box? How long was he in that box? No, it don't bear thinking of.

Just the same, she had to think of it, and the thought was so wretched that she stood up, clambered past the sack of coins and started walking fast. I wonder which is the worst of those three? The old duchess is even nastier than my ma—which is saying a good deal; and young Lot is just about as stupid and spiteful as they come— and a drunk, as well; and as for that Baron Magnus, if I had to choose between him and a snake for company on a desert island, I know which I'd pick.

Far in the distance she heard the lift creak.

Odds cuss it, thought Dido, now what'll I do? If it's Lot on his own I reckon I can dodge him. I can play hide-and-seek down here in this rabbit warren of a place as well as he can—probably better, drunk as he is. But suppose he's brought some of those Black Hoods down with him?

She strained her ears, listening. A small amount of

188

time went by—five minutes, perhaps. Then Dido began to hear voices. I might as well get to hear what they're saying, she thought.

Strangely enough, the voices did not come from behind her, where the lift was, but somewhere ahead. The narrow, twisting passage made the sounds echo confusingly, but she was fairly sure of the general direction. Blowing out her candle, she crept softly along, guiding herself by touching the wooden wine racks on either side; there was just room for a smallish person to pass between them.

Now the wine racks gave way to damp brick walls— Dido could feel moss growing between the bricks—and the passage sloped quite steeply downhill. Also the air began to feel cold, and then colder, and then very cold indeed. And a faint bluish light began to glimmer ahead. Lord a mussy, thought Dido, what the pink blazes am I getting into?

But curiosity urged her on. The voices were louder now. The darkness changed to flickering twilight. And suddenly she found a cold metal railing barring her way. She stood still, clutching the rail and looking down at a strange scene.

Below her lay a huge vaulted chamber the size of a small cathedral. The walls, which curved up into an arched roof, were of brick. Looking sideways, Dido could see other entrances besides hers, some higher, some lower, like gulls' nests in a cliff. The air was bitterly, bitterly cold. And this was because of the white substance that filled the great space up to a level only a few feet below where Dido stood. The white substance was ice.

Dido now remembered that, when they were up in the attic, Piers had told her something about the icehouses, several of them, that lay underneath Fogrum Hall. "When Lady Adelaide's grandfather lived here, they used to chop the ice out of the lake when it froze in winter and store it in the icehouses for ice puddings and drinks in summer. And Baron Magnus had ice fetched when there was that cold spell last month—something to do with the Black Pilgrimage, I heard him tell Her Grace the duchess. . . ."

Shivering, Dido looked down at the huge circular floor of white. There was a ladder attached to the wall below her leading down to it. The other entrances, she guessed, were for when the ice level was higher or lower. At present the great storeroom seemed about half full.

Somebody—a person—was lying on a couch, ringed by about fifty burning candles, in the middle of the ice. And the boy, Lot, was leaning over the safety rail of another entrance, waving a brandy bottle and shouting raucously,

"Hey, Dad! *Dad!* You gotta listen to me! You gotta listen!"

He's wholly drunk now, thought Dido; that boy is as stoned as a newt.

"Dad! You must listen to me! Dido Twite's cut loose and she's somewhere down here. If we don't collar her, she'll do something bad—pinch all our grog maybe. She'll find a way out. *Dad*, d'you hear what I'm saying?"

After a long pause the figure on the couch spoke.

How can he stand it down there on the ice? Dido thought.

"How dare you, boy? How *dare* you come down here disturbing me when you know my rules?"

Dido thought, I sure wouldn't want someone to speak to me in that voice.

"But, Dad! It's really, really important! She probably knows where the king is." Lot took another swig from his bottle.

"Wretched boy! You have brought my soul back. From the dead city. From Chorazim, where they wait for the Third Coming. You brought me back before my time there was done. How can I work my revenge if you bring me back? Three human hearts were needed to start me on my journey, and you—you poor fool—must come trespassing."

"Trespassing!" yelled Lot in a fury. "You forget who *I* am! I'm the queen's son! They wouldn't put *you* on the throne! Half mad, half wild beast—and shut up in the Tower fifteen years for a lot of murders. . . ."

Used as she was to bad language from her father and his associates, Dido shook with shock at the venomous stream of curses that now issued from the figure on the couch. She supposed it must be the baron, though he was strangely bandaged up, like a mummy, like a dead person. Dido could not imagine how he endured lying

191

there just a few inches above that deadly cold floor. And he'd been here since yesterday, she reckoned, if he had come down here when he'd left the room saying he was going on the Black Pilgrimage. What did he mean, "Three human hearts were needed"? Did he kill three people? I sure am glad no one has noticed me up here.

She was even more relieved next moment when a new voice broke in.

"You may as well hold your peace, Magnus Rudh, Cantacuzelos Albecchini! For your luck is running out."

"*Luck?* What luck have I ever had? Shut up in that vile prison, obliged to be civil to that dolt of a doctor, insulted, traduced—and for what? Because that man wanted my wife! He didn't have her for long! And what in perdition are *you* doing here—hell hag! Serpent!"

"Come to pay a neighborly visit. And to ask a question."

Dido, peering sideways from her doorway, could get no more than a glimpse of the person who was speaking to Magnus. She was tall and female, judging by her voice and the triangular white headdress she wore.

"That sack of sixpences will be your undoing, Magnus, old enemy from the past," she went on composedly. "That and your loving children. What a pair! Your son can't wait to be rid of you, and your daughter is at this very time setting up the process for your annihilation."

"My daughter? That worthless hussy? What has *she* got to say to anything?"

"She is angry, resentful because she hoped you would give her a father's loving welcome."

"Why should I? What did she ever do for me?"

"What indeed? And all she can do you now is harm. But I could prevent that, Magnus, brother, if in return you could tell me something."

"Why should I stir a finger for you?" he snarled.

"Why? To save yourself from a very unpleasant fate. But that is up to you! You have failed—have you not— in your attempt to reach Chorazim and regain your former strength."

Lot, who had occupied the past few minutes in swallowing copious gulps from his bottle, now upended it and threw it down on the ice with a crash.

"Ask me," he bawled, "the Dad's no more use than a wooden ship's figurehead. Black Pilgrimage, indeed! *Hic!* That's three useful workboys from the school he went and killed—and for what? So's he could—*hic!*— have a nap on the ice for three days. Aunt Minna thinks he's a total loss."

"Oh, be quiet, you horrible sot!" snapped the lady in the headdress. "You should hear what your aunt Minna thinks of *you*. . . . Listen, Magnus: Your wife, my cousin Adelaide, when she married Prince Richard of Wales, had a desk, which she left behind in Fogrum Hall. Do you happen to know where that desk might be?"

Silence from the figure on the ice.

"Do you know where that desk is?" the lady repeated.

Ho! thought Dido. *He* may not know where that desk

is, but I know. But what's in it that's worth such a lot? Worth saving his life for? There was naught in the desk but an old diary. That ain't summat to make a song and dance about. Is it?

Lot, evidently not at all interested in his mother's desk and its contents, now withdrew, apparently to help himself to another bottle. But in a moment he was back in a state of boozy excitement.

"I say! Here's a go! Some of the wine racks are alight! There's a bonfire burning back there! You best hoist yourself up smartish, Dad, if you don't want to be toasted like a sardine—and you too, Aunt Titania. Ha ha ha! That'd be a lark, wouldn't it? I'm off, lickety-split!"

In fact Dido, turning to look back, saw a red glow behind her and smelt a strong hot smell of burning wood and alcohol. Mercy, she thought, there's enough stingo back there to make this place hotter than a smith's forge. I reckon it's time for me to make an exit too.

The passage behind her was blocked with gouts of flame and puffs of black smoke. But in front of her was the ladder leading down onto the ice. She ducked under the rail and clambered silently down. She noticed that Baron Magnus was slowly rising to his feet and unwinding his white wrappings. He did not notice Dido, nor did Lot, who was dancing about singing, "This old man, he played one, he played nick-nack on my rum, nick-nack-paddywack, give a dog a bone, this old man he won't get home!"

Silent and unremarked, Dido skirted round the side of

the great ice-filled chamber, keeping in the shadows, far distant from Baron Magnus and his ring of candles.

Opposite the ladder she had come down, she found another, leading to another, larger entrance above. Maybe this is where they bring the ice from the lake, she thought. Maybe I can get out this way. She began to climb the ladder but, when halfway up it, was arrested by a fearful shriek. She turned to see something that would haunt her for years to come.

Magnus had been slowly, clumsily hoisting himself up a ladder. The one I came down, Dido thought. His movements were vague and uncoordinated, as if he were only half awake. But when he was just a few rungs from the top, a thin stream of silvery molten metal came spurting out of the entrance above him, splashed down on him and completely coated him with a glistening layer. Flames instantly burst from him and he burned like a torch. One moment Dido saw him on the ladder; next minute there was nothing left of him or the ladder but a black filmy wisp, which blew away across the ice.

Stunned, Dido pulled herself up into the dark entrance above.

chapter fourteen

THE PASSAGE THAT Dido had taken to escape from the ice chamber was far wider than the one by which she had entered. Carts loaded with ice from the lake could have driven along it. After ten minutes' fast trotting, she felt confident enough to relight her candle. She was hollow with hunger, as she had eaten nothing since those cucumber sandwiches with the archbishop; she was desperately tired and shocked. But still a faint spark of hope burned in her heart, for at least she was alone and free and perhaps on a track that would lead her out of Fogrum Hall and away from its dreadful inhabitants. What would happen to Lot? Would he escape the fire or die in it like his horrible father? And that old girl? Who could she be? She had addressed Baron Magnus as brother, so she must be connected—unless of course she was just being sarcastic.

What a crew, thought Dido. I hope I never run into any of 'em ever again. She was horribly disconcerted to be addressed by a voice that hailed her from close behind.

"*Dido?* Are you Dido Twite?"

A figure drew out of the dark, caught up and ran beside her. Glancing sideways, Dido saw that it was a girl, perhaps her own age. Dark hair and bright eyes could be seen in the candlelight, that was all.

"What's it to you who I am?" Dido said gruffly.

"Oh, don't worry! I am not going to give you up to my odious father and brother. They can burn to death for all I care. And I hope they do."

Then she don't know what already happened to her da, Dido thought.

"I hate them both! That's why I brought a witch bottle to put under the house. It cost a lot but it was worth it."

Blimey, thought Dido. She sure is a cool one. What about the other folk in the house? Don't they have a say?

"What about the old lady?" she asked. "The one he called a hell hag?"

"Was there an old lady? I don't know anything about her," the girl said carelessly. "My name's Jorinda, by the way. Jorinda Coldacre. You know Simon Bakerloo, don't you?"

"Kind of," Dido said cautiously.

"I'm going to marry him," the girl announced.

Dido gasped, but kept her thoughts to herself. They were far from happy.

"So that's why I want Simon to be king, and not my stupid brother."

"*Could* S-Simon be king?"

"Oh, yes. If the old king dies and gives Simon Alfred's crown, it's a dead cert."

"I see."

"At first," the girl confided, "I was on the side of the Burgundians."

"Oh?"

"Aunt Minna, the duchess of Burgundy, is bringing them over. They are going to land at Marshport and march on London and put my brother on the throne. And then I'd be the king's sister. But I think it's better if I marry Simon and then I'd be queen. Don't you think so?"

"If—if Simon likes the idea?"

"Oh, he will. I *really* love him," said the girl dreamily. "Really, really! Oh, it's good talking to you, Dido! It's so good to have a friend, somebody to come right into my world! The girls at school were stupid, and the people at Coldacre are all lower class and can't enter into my sentiments and aspirations. My grandfather is pro-Burgundian because they buy his sheep and he used to dance with the duchess long ago at Almacks's assembly rooms, but *I* think Aunt Minna is an old horror—don't you?—and I expect if the Burgundians don't find the sheep waiting for them at Marshport, they will just get into their ships and sail back to Burgundy. Don't you suppose that is what they'll do?"

"What do they want the sheep for?"

"To eat. I'm a vegetarian," said the girl. "Are you? What's your favorite food?"

"Cucumber sandwiches."

"Oh, famous! But now the problem is: First, where is the king? And, second, where's Alfred's crown? Do you know where they are?"

"Nope," said Dido. "Neither of them. Not the foggiest."

"Someone said the crown might be in Queen Adelaide's desk. But nobody seems to know where that is."

Dido kept her thoughts to herself.

"Of course *my* mamma was not Queen Adelaide," the girl went on chattily. "My horrible father was married twice. Or at least he had two wives. My mamma was Zoe Coldacre . . . but she died when I was born. So Lot is only my half brother. And we don't know yet if either of us is going to take after Papa."

"Take after him?"

"He was a werewolf, you know. That was why he was shut up in the Tower of London for fifteen years. He thought it was wholly unfair. Why should he be shut up for something he couldn't help?"

"I heard about him," said Dido cautiously. "But hadn't he killed a lot of folk?"

"Well, he couldn't help that! That's what werewolves do. That was done during the times when he was a wolf. At night, you know. So Lot and I don't yet know if that is going to happen to us. It sometimes happens when you are about twenty-one."

"How will you know?"

"The first sign is, you can't see yourself in the mirror. Oh, *wouldn't* it be exciting!"

"Did you know Lord Herodsfoot?" Dido asked.

"Why?"

"I jist wondered."

"I saw him once or twice," the girl said casually. "He collected games for the king, didn't he? He had a game called Brooks on the Moon, or something like that; he thought it might cheer the king up, distract him, cure him of whatever is the matter with him. Of course Pa didn't want that. Herodsfoot wasn't a bad old stick. Pa shut him up in a box, Lot told me, because he wouldn't tell where the king was. Maybe he really didn't know. I didn't think he'd be dead for so long, not for *ever*. I was sorry when Lot told me that."

Dido did not ask whether Jorinda had known the Woodlouse. They were now approaching the end of the long tunnel, which had led them up a gradual incline for about half a mile. Ahead of them they could see a circle of pale sky; the night was coming to an end.

Woodlouse and Herodsfoot, thought Dido, I'll not forget you. Not ever. Not ever. That's about all I can do for ye.

An iron gate barred the entrance to the tunnel. But Jorinda had a key.

"I nicked it off the park keeper," she explained. "I used to come and stay for half-term sometimes."

She also had a dapple-gray pony, which—luckily for the pony—she had tethered inside the gate. Luckily, for they discovered that outside a severe blizzard was raging. Snow blew in long white streamers, sideways, across a vista of lake, clumps of tall trees and rolling parkland.

"What a dismal nuisance," said Jorinda. "It's going to take me forever to ride to Coldacre in this. Goodbye, Dido. I really enjoyed talking to you. Oh . . . you might as well have this. An Eccles cake. I brought it for my brother; Lot loves cake. But I never saw him, so you can have it."

She reached down from her pony's back and handed Dido a small solid circular cake wrapped in tissue paper.

"Eat it for your breakfast! Goodbye!"

She kicked her heels into the pony's flanks and rode off into the snowstorm at a smart canter.

Dido gazed after her, long and thoughtfully, until she had disappeared in the driving snow. Then she looked down at the small clammy object in her hand.

Dido was not fond of cake. And, although hungry, she did not at all fancy this one. Unwrapped, it was both sticky and greasy, a shell of bright yellow pastry wrapped around a mass of little black wrinkled things. Were they currants? Perhaps. They looked thoroughly unappetizing. Dido broke off a quarter of the cake and dropped it on the snowy grass. Two small wild birds had been sheltering inside the tunnel entrance. They pounced on the pastry, pecked at it eagerly—and both fell dead among the crumbs.

"Humph," said Dido. "Sorry about that, birdies! I wondered why she should take the trouble to bring a cake to her brother, for she didn't seem so all-fired fond of him. I reckon the rest of this can go down among the fishes."

She walked to the border of the lake, which was close at hand, dropped the cake into the water, noticing that a film of ice was beginning to form along the edge, and knelt to rinse her hands in the freezing water.

"Now, which way do we go? Too bad Miss Jorinda didn't wait to give me any directions. But I reckon if she had, they'd only lead me into trouble."

Since Dido had no idea where in England Fogrum Hall was situated, nor where the nearest town lay, her simplest course was to walk away from the house, which also had the advantage of keeping the wind at her back.

And no one's likely to see me in this weather, she thought. Also, they've other things to worry about.

Peering behind her through ribbons of snow, she could see a dense black plume of smoke blowing her way over a tree-covered hillock out of which the tunnel emerged. Maybe they'll blame me for the fire, Dido thought. I'd best get away as fast as I can manage.

This was not very fast. Besides hunger and exhaustion, she now had worry. Was it possible that that awful girl was really going to marry Simon? Or was it just something she hoped for? Dido had not seen Simon for a good many months while she had been away in America; all sorts of things could happen in a short time. Here was the poor king apparently about to die, and David the prince of Wales dead in some catastrophe in the north, but did that really mean Simon was next in line to the throne? Could that be possible?

Struggling on through the storm, Dido hoped devoutly that Simon had too much good sense to marry a girl who was capable of poisoning her own brother. Did he know how ruthless she was? Could he be aware that her father was a werewolf and her brother a drunkard?

Dido was making her way across a huge park with rough grass, scattered trees and patches of woodland. As she trudged on she began to see that the park boundary ahead of her was a wall, a twenty-foot-high barrier that seemed to run on and on without a break. But there had been a gateway. Dido remembered the arrival of the carriage and the two stone gateposts with crumbling griffins on them. What a long time ago that arrival now seemed. What a lot had happened at Fogrum Hall.

This park, she thought, is as big as Ameriky. I hope I don't have another hundred miles to walk before I find a gate.

With relief, after a while, she saw a gap ahead, and a small lodge building beside it, set about with tall trees. The gap contained a gate, but the gate was shut. What's the odds that it's locked, thought Dido, and I'll have to tell some tale to make them let me out? That is, if there's anybody at home in the lodge.

However, as she neared the lodge, its door opened and a man came out. He wore a black robe and hood, which made Dido's heart sink. Croopus, is he one of the baron's strong-arm boys?

As the man walked toward the gate, while Dido was still about twenty yards away, an unexpected thing happened. A massive branch broke from one of the big trees by the lodge, and it blew straight down toward the man.

"Hey, *mister*!" yelled Dido. "Watch out!"

He did not hear. He had not seen her. Her voice was drowned by the gale. She raced toward him and just managed to tug him backward as the branch smashed down onto the spot where he had been. Dido and the man both fell to the ground in a tangle of twigs and leaves, but otherwise unhurt.

The lodge door shot open and an aproned woman scudded out.

"Oh, Your Reverence! Are you killt? Are you hurt bad? Oh my lordy-lord, what a thing to happen . . . just when you've been so good, visiting my poor Tim!"

"No, Mrs. Dale, I am quite unharmed, thank you, due to the speedy action of this excellent young person."

The elderly man struggled to his feet and Dido saw with immense relief that he was a clergyman, not one of the baron's henchmen. "Your Tim will have his work cut out, sawing up that bough for firewood, when he is back on his feet, which I trust will be in a day or two. No, truly, I am perfectly unhurt, Mrs. Dale, and must be on my way without delay. Ah, thank you, thank you," he said as the woman ran to open the gate for him and Dido, then shut and bolted it behind them.

"I think you saved my life," the man then said politely to Dido. "Shall we exchange names? I am Father Sam, of Saint Arling's Chapel. Who are you and where are you bound?"

Dido liked the look of Father Sam and replied without hesitation, "I'm Dido Twite, mister, and I'm not just sure where I'm going, because I haven't the foggiest notion where I am . . . but I'm looking for a chap called Simon Bakerloo."

The man's face lit up. "Bless my soul! What a piece of good fortune! I am on my way this very minute to meet that very Simon! He asked if I knew your whereabouts. I saw him only a few hours ago and told him how to find his way to Otherland Priory, where I hope he may be now. He had hoped to take refuge in my hermitage, but that was not possible, for it was in imminent danger of flooding . . . and I had to go on a charitable errand."

"Oh, mister! Oh, Father Sam! What a lucky thing! Is Simon a-going to see the king? I just been in Fogrum Hall, where there's a batch of jammy-fingered coves 'ud give their ears and whiskers for a buzz about where His Nibs has got to —"

"Hush, my child! Walls have ears!" Father Sam exclaimed, glancing at the high park wall. "Let us get away from this neighborhood."

"I'm right with you there, Reverence," Dido agreed.

Dense forest skirted the park wall on its outer side, beyond a narrow coach road. Father Sam glanced this way and that, evidently searching for a landmark, then found a notched yew tree and plunged unhesitatingly into the woods. Dido, following him, discovered that a narrow path, out of sight of the carriageway, ran steeply downhill between the trees.

"The road goes round," Father Sam explained to Dido, "but the path goes across. It is a shortcut. But the floods will prevent our following it all the way. We shall have to leave it after a few miles and skirt round the flooded area. Still, it will save us an hour's walking. And if—but how in the world did you come to be in Fogrum Hall, child?"

"I was scrobbled, Father." Dido explained how she had been kidnapped after her interview with the archbishop and what had happened after that.

"I see. . . . So you will not be aware that His Grace the archbishop was found murdered a couple of days ago?"

"No! Is that so? Poor old boy! Now, who would do in a decent old cove like that?"

"Oh, unquestionably it was done by order of Baron Magnus. Some guards at the Tower—and a doctor—were also found with their throats slit. Doubtless Baron Magnus had a grudge against them."

"I reckon he had a grudge against almost everybody . . . except maybe that fat old duchess. Too bad she's still around. And Lot—his son—we don't know if he was done for in the fire or if he's still live and kicking."

"Hark!" Father Sam held up a finger. Through the trees above them on the hillside came the rattle of a carriage being driven at a gallop. And, a moment later, the sound of a single horse, ridden at the same headlong pace.

"D'you reckon that might be someone after me?" asked Dido uneasily.

"It is possible. You might have been seen crossing the park. Or they might have asked at the lodge. But if so," said Father Sam comfortably, "you have now given them the slip. A carriage can't follow you down this path. And the snow is covering our footprints."

"Father," said Dido after a while, "what d'you reckon those things are, on ahead?"

They had come to a scantily wooded stretch of forest, where the ground was covered with fern and bracken now beaten down by the snow into sodden lumps. Among these tussocks were half a hundred human figures, seated, silent and motionless. They wore green-and-gray jackets. The snow had crowned them with white caps. They were apparently alive but seemed to be unconscious. The oddest thing about them was that they were all seated six to twelve inches above the ground.

"Holy custard!" said Dido. "How d'you reckon they do that, Father?"

Father Sam was worried.

"Oh, dear me! They will very soon freeze to death if we leave them like that. I am afraid it is certainly my duty to help them. If you will just give me a hand, my dear, I think we can soon rouse them."

chapter fifteen

OTHERLAND PRIORY OCCUPIED what had once been a dark strip of barren land on the edge of the coast but separated from the mainland by the Middle Mere, a long, narrow freshwater pool, reputed to be bottomless. Over centuries the monks of the Priory had cultivated the strip of land, creating vineyards, orchards, gardens and fields of corn where there had been nothing but a rock-crowned hummock of sand. In flood time or at spring tides, it was cut off, and at all times it was inaccessible except to those who knew their way through the mazy swamplands, the clumps of willow and alder whose roots were exposed at low tide, the beds of reeds and rushes, the slow-moving streams that changed their courses from week to week. Mist often lay among the islets for weeks on end; flocks of wading birds, swans, pelicans, herons and storks, inhabited the channels.

There were quicksands into which unwary travelers had sunk and never been seen again.

On the seaward side of Otherland a shingle bank, twenty miles long and forty feet high, ran from the Priory down to Wan Hope Point. Ships were often wrecked on this bank, as the currents that swept down it were fierce and treacherous. Local shipping knew better than to come anywhere near the coast thereabouts, but generations of wreckers had lit bonfires on the shingle bank—which was known as Querck Bank—to entice strange ships to their doom.

King Richard's grandfather, Angus the Silent, had decreed that the railway be extended from Marshport to the Priory land so that the cargoes and wreckage from foundered ships could be transported inland. "Otherwise," he said, "yon canny monks get it all!" This was true, and the railway was begun. But, due to one reason and another, it was never finished during the lifetime of King Angus, and since then, funds to finish it were not forthcoming. A grand viaduct had originally been built, connecting the highest point on the mainland with the rocky crag that formed the pinnacle of Otherland Mount, but the rail track had never been laid across the viaduct and the rubble bedding of the track had been much worn away by the passage of time. Few chose to approach Otherland on foot by that route; the dizzy height of the viaduct, two hundred and fifty feet, was enough to deter most people, and then there was a dauntingly steep climb down at the seaward end.

On Father Sam's advice, Simon had chosen this approach to Otherland because floodwater had greatly increased the width of the marshy channel down below; in any case there did not seem to be any ferryboat, and if there had been, he did not see how the sedan chair was to be loaded into a boat.

But now, within a stone's throw of the entrance to the viaduct, he was starting to have grave doubts as to the wisdom of this choice. In fact he was beginning to think he had made a terrible mistake. Old Harry was not encouraging.

"We'll niver get t'old gentleman across yon footway!" he lamented. "Niver! I've come as far as my old pins'll bear me, Mester Simon; they 'on't take me across yon devil's causeway, I'm telling you! Nor the sheep don't like it, neether, Mester Simon. Look at them!"

It was true. The sheep did look very dispirited. Many of them were lying down on the snowy rail bed; others were dismally nibbling at bits of bramble and brushwood that sprouted along the gritty side of the permanent way. And Simon's latest protégés, a pair of Russian bears, were hunkered down with their heads sunk between their shoulders, and forepaws dangling, the very picture of dejection.

"I do wish Father Sam had caught up with us," Simon said.

Father Sam had given Simon excellent directions for skirting as quickly as possible round the flooded forest.

"But when ye get to the Middle Mere, there's a

211

problem," he had said. "Ye'd never find your own way through the waterways; ye'd have to find a boatman. And the boatmen may be paddling any otherwhere in the floods, the way things are just now. So you'd best take the high way. I'll come up with ye as fast as I can but I've a couple of sick folk to visit—ye can't disappoint sick folk—and I'm afeered those boys in the URSA may be needing medical advice. But I'll haste after ye as fast as I'm able; we'd best meet at the end of the viaduct, where the permanent way runs out of Wanmeeting Wood."

So that was where Simon was now waiting with his companions.

And that was where Jorinda found him. She was riding a hired horse, a bay hack, which started and shied at sight of the bears, so she reined in at the edge of the wood, dismounted and tied her horse to a tree.

"So *this* is where you've got to!" she said. "Aunt Minna thought as much. Do you know that you can be seen on the skyline? Clearly! Not very sensible, was it? Aunt Titania said that was what you would do. Now that my father is dead, they will probably support your claim to the throne. What on *earth* are you doing to that bear?"

Simon was massaging its ears.

"The damp air gives them a headache," he said. "They are used to a dry winter cold."

The bear was wagging its head to and fro, evidently getting considerable relief from Simon's massage. Its mate sat nearby, patiently waiting to be treated.

"I suppose you have got the king hidden in that

sedan chair," Jorinda said. "Wretched old man. Is he still alive?"

"Hold thy tongue, miss," growled Harry, who had taken a strong dislike to Jorinda, " 'tis no business of yourn."

"Well, it is if I'm going to help you," she said. "I'm on your side, now Pa's dead. And I'm sure you shouldn't stay with the king in this drafty spot. The Burgundians are sure to land very soon and there will probably be a battle. You had best get the king into shelter so you can go through the coronet ritual. I suppose you *have* got King Alfred's coronet? Besides, it's getting colder all the time."

Simon did not wish to explain to this tiresome girl that they were waiting for Father Sam. He did not wish to tell her anything at all. He wished strongly that she would go away. Much of what she said was true, and he wished it were not.

"Those are my grandfather's sheep, aren't they?" she said. "The ones he sold to the Burgundians. You took them. The Burgundians will be in a rage about that."

"I paid for the sheep," Simon said, moving over to the second bear, which rubbed its great heavy head lovingly against him. "They were being disgracefully ill treated. Where is your cat?"

"Oh, it got killed," Jorinda answered carelessly. "My father killed it. He couldn't stand animals. By the way, I saw your friend Dido Twite this morning. She was in my father's house."

213

"You saw Dido?"

"At Fogrum Hall, yes. I've no idea what she was do-ing, or how she got there."

"*When* was this?"

"Oh, today. Early. I gave her a cake." For some reason she giggled. Simon accidentally pulled the bear's ear. It turned and bit him, but gently.

"What was Dido doing there?"

Jorinda was tempted to say, "She was running away after setting fire to the house," but something about Simon's manner, his piercing look, made her too nervous to lie.

"Where did you get the bears?" she asked hastily.

"*What was Dido doing at Fogrum Hall?*"

"I really haven't the faintest idea! Those bears belong to the Burgundians, don't they? Aunt Minna ordered them by mistake."

"Aunt Minna. Who is that?"

"The duchess of Burgundy. I had lunch with her and Aunt T in Clarion Wells. Aunt Minna said the food at Fogrum Hall was disgusting, so she moved to the Royal Hotel. That was before the fire. And then, while we were having lunch, her majordomo came in and told her that Pa had died in an accident; he was burned in a stream of molten silver. Not very nice, was it?" Jorinda shivered a little. "Aunt Minna *was* planning to put Lot on the throne, but I think she's changed her mind. Have you got Alfred's coronet?"

With a strong effort, Simon prevented himself from glancing anxiously toward the sedan chair. Father Sam had provided the king with several hot bricks and had administered a warm posset of eggs, honey, mead and horse chestnut, which, he said, would be beneficial for the patient's blood flow and would help him to sleep on the journey. It had worked well. But where *was* Father Sam? Why didn't he come? Soon the sun would set — not that the sun had ever been visible that day; gusts of wind still hurled snow in all directions. And how they were ever to get the sedan chair across the viaduct without Father Sam's help Simon could not conceive.

"When you and I are married," Jorinda said to Simon, "I can tell you I shan't allow a lot of *animals* in our house. Animals are nothing but a messy nuisance."

Simon's jaw dropped. He stared at the girl in utter astonishment. The very last thing in the world he wanted was to be married to this person.

"Who said anything about our getting married?"

She gave him her long, long sparkling look.

"I did! It will be wonderful! You'll see! We must get married! We'll make the handsomest couple in the English Isles!"

At this moment a mournful cry came from the sedan chair.

"Help! Help me! Where is everybody?"

And Simon's owl, Thunderbolt, came flapping hurriedly from the window slot.

"Oh, murder!" said Simon.

"Oh, my laws, Mester Simon!" cried old Harry. "Look there! Now what are we a-going to do?"

He pointed to where the rail bed ran out of Wanmeeting Wood. A rider on a black horse was galloping along it toward them.

"Oh, no!" cried Jorinda in dismay. "That's my wretched brother, Lot! I hoped he was dead. Go away, Lot! Go right away, you horrible beast! Nobody wants you here!"

"You hold your stupid tongue!" yelled Lot. "Nobody wants *you* anywhere at all!"

Seen close to, Lot looked dreadful. Apparently he had escaped from the fire at Fogrum Hall, but not without being quite badly burned; half his face and his left arm were dark red, his clothes were black tatters and the hair on the left side of his head was singed to stubble. He was clutching one of the Saxon fighters' green spears, and he galloped his horse straight at Simon, who was standing beside the sedan chair.

"I always hated you, Battersea!" he shouted. "You filthy scum. I'll lay it was you who burned down my house!"

He flung himself off the horse and drove his spear hard at Simon, who jumped aside. But as he did so, Jorinda threw herself in between her brother and Simon. She received the spear full in her throat and died instantly.

Cursing and grunting with fury, Lot struggled to drag

the spear back out of Jorinda's throat, but while he was trying to do this, one of the bears came and wrapped its great furred clawed arms round him.

"Let go of me! I'll kill you; I'll get you!" shouted Lot, apparently unaware that his adversary was not human.

At this moment a carriage and pair came rattling along the rail bed and two ladies precipitated themselves from it.

"Lothar! Lothar!" they screamed. "What are you doing there? Come back at once, at once! Control yourself!"

Simon, staggering to his feet, stared at the women in disbelief. One of them was large and stout; he guessed her to be the duchess of Burgundy. The other was the lady Titania.

She took no notice of Simon. All her attention was focused on Lot.

"Lothar! Listen to me! Stop shouting! Leave that bear alone and come here. Stop shouting! *Calm yourself.*"

"That piece of scum burned down my house!"

"Ridiculous rubbish. Your own sister did that."

The bear let go of Lot, who lurched to his feet, staring at the two ladies.

"Your aunt Titania is right," announced the duchess severely. "If you are hoping to be king, Lothar, you must learn to control yourself." She stared with deep disapproval at the body of Jorinda. "Did you do that? Answer me! Stop cursing and swearing, take a deep breath and *come here!*"

217

But Lot did not obey her. He did not answer. He was changing, in a silent, visible and terrifying manner. His teeth were becoming fangs; they grew longer and longer. His eyes blazed. His hands stretched and narrowed into paws with long claws. Thick dark fur sprouted over his face and neck.

He began moving slowly, menacingly toward the two women, who cried out in alarm and scrambled back into their carriage. The horses, screaming in terror, galloped off wildly along the viaduct, with the carriage lurching and swaying behind them. Lot vengefully pursued it. The viaduct parapet was no more than knee height. One extra-violent lurch of the carriage sent the whole rig over the embankment; Lot, who had just hurled himself at one of the horses, went with it.

Next minute a distant crash and splash came from far below.

"Lord a mercy!" breathed old Harry. He and Simon stared at each other in silent consternation. Then Simon went, almost mechanically, to soothe Lothar's black horse and tether it beside his own mare.

"What's happening? What in the world is going on?" called the king piteously from behind his curtain.

"We had a bit of trouble, Your Majesty," called Simon. "With Lothar."

"Cousin Dick! Cousin Dick!"

"Cousin Dick. But the trouble is over, thank heaven." Simon opened the flap of the sedan chair and did his best to give the king a reassuring smile. Then he turned round to see Harry, with a certain amount of effort, lift Jorinda's body and push it over the parapet. There was another splash and crack of breaking ice.

"Oh, dear," said Simon. "Was that the right thing to do?"

"Best she should join her brother," grunted Harry. "She were a no-good wench. A real hussy. Thinking to marry you! What next? And as for him . . ."

"But she was killed defending me."

"Only accidental. She never helped another body in her life, 'less 'twas by mistake. Don't waste your sorrow on her. What we got to worry about is how to get Himself down to the Priory afore darkfall."

"And in good time," exclaimed Simon, "here comes Father Sam!" He peered through the curtain of snow, which was falling faster now. His voice almost cracked with astonishment and joy. "Father Sam and Dido!"

chapter sixteen

DIDO WALKED SLOWLY down the hill beside the sedan chair. She had undone the leather curtain so that the king could see out, and she was holding a slow and disjointed conversation with him.

"Do I know you?"

"I carried your train at Your Majesty's coronation. A fine affair it was. All those oranges dangling on the pillars of Saint Paul's—"

"Oh, do call me Uncle Dick, my dear girl."

"Sure, if you say so, Your Maj—Uncle Dick—and the congregation all munching on almond cookies—"

"And, havers, I'd no say no tae one o' they almond cakies at this present."

"Maybe they'll have some over yonder," said Dido hopefully, scanning the spiky outline of the monastery perched on its mount, fitfully glimpsed through gusts of snow.

Lot's black horse had been harnessed between the two rear carrying poles; the poor beast was so tired and shocked that it offered no resistance to this unusual arrangement, did not even take fright at the two bears who padded companionably alongside. The sheep, docile and humble, trailed in the rear, and old Harry rode Simon's Magpie. Simon and Father Sam bore the two front carrying poles, and the whole party proceeded at a cautious and creeping pace down the zigzag path, which was both steep and slippery. The gale had not abated; driven snow scoured their faces and their goal seemed a daunting distance away across a wide expanse of island-studded white flatness, which appeared and disappeared behind clouds of sleet and spume.

Father Sam was explaining to Simon why it had taken him such a long time to make his way to the viaduct.

"The Saxon Army, poor dear fellows, their commander Egbert Wetwulf is so very much taken up with what they call 'reflection prowess'—a very worthy tactic I am sure it is, very worthy indeed, never a doubt of that—it puts the whole army in thought accord with one another, hardly any need for speech, they tell me, and of course that is excellent, excellent; it turns them truly into a band of brothers. But, ye see, while they are, as they call it, *reflecting*—they sit cross-legged and pass into a deep, deep trance; some of them even levitate, rise a little way into the air — but that, d'ye see, means they are somewhat immune to outside influences; they hardly see nor hear. *Well!* So there they all were! And I could see that if they were not roused from that insensibility, they might very likely freeze to death in such weather as we are having. And if the Burgundians were to arrive at such a time — it hardly bears thinking of. So I felt it my duty . . ."

"A good thing you did," Simon agreed. "I suppose Lothar must have grabbed one of their spears as he rode by. I wonder how he knew we would come this way?"

"I imagine Lady Titania Plantagenet must have told him."

"Why? I thought she was on the king's side, devoted to him."

"She has — had — the gift of augury."

"What's that?"

"Foretelling what is going to happen. She must have known what would come to pass . . . up to a point at least. Your young friend has it too."

"Dido has? I don't get it."

"*Not* a comfortable gift," said Father Sam, shaking his head. "At present, in Dido it is only latent . . . like that wretched boy with his wolf persona. He, at least, is no loss. Nor his scatterbrained sister. A pity she had not come across the Saxon Army. She would have done better with them. A set of excellent, high-minded lads. I told them it was their duty to go and argue with the Burgundians before engaging in warfare and they agreed to try that method. . . ."

"Is that the railway up there?" the king asked Dido. "Do you think I could be in time to catch the five-thirty train to Back End Junction, where I might change and get the express to King's Cross?"

Dido was cautious.

"I wouldn't depend on that, your Maj—Uncle Richard, sir. If I was you, I'd stay overnight at the Priory. I daresay the monks in that place are a very decent set of welcoming fellers and will cook you a fine dinner."

She certainly hoped so. It seemed like a hundred years since those cucumber sandwiches.

The king was anxious and melancholy.

"Do I belong here?"

"Not here, perhaps, Your Royalness, but soon we'll find where you do belong."

"I have left myself behind—"

"You'll find yourself, I reckon, when you're in a nice bedroom with a cup of hot soup inside you. . . ."

"My dear . . . I wonder if you can advise me. I feel I am very close to my latter end. What I chiefly wish to know is this: In the next world I shall find my two dear wives waiting: my dearest Edelgarde, the mother of Davie, and my equally dear Adelaide. Now, shall I have to introduce them to each other? Or will they have become known to each other already? And what about my son?"

Dido gave this some careful thought.

"Don't you reckon, Your Maj—Uncle Dick—that everybody knows everything, once they get there? And don't need to be told nothing?"

223

"Yes. Yes . . . I believe you may be right. I do hope so. That would take a great weight off my mind. Another question that troubles me: this religious establishment whither we are tending. Do you ken if they harbor any nightingales in their policies?"

"Policies?"

"Estates, demesnes—"

"You got me there, Uncle King. But—even spose they have nightingales—ain't they birds that sing in summertime? Not very likely they'd be yodeling around in weather like this."

"Oh," said the king sadly. "I wonder if you are right."

Dido wondered why His Majesty had such a wish for nightingales. Something to do, perhaps, with that business the old archbishop had been clacking on about— the coronet ritual? Mercy, what a long time ago that seems, thought Dido, the old gager and his tea things in his spooky little hidey-hole on the bank of London River. Only a few days ago . . .

She was reminded of the archbishop's riverside retreat, because they had now arrived at just such another bankside area—a dank willowy neighborhood with clumps of reeds and bulrush and a wooden slipway running down under the flat white surface of snow-covered ice. There was a tumbledown open-fronted shed, with a bench, under a clump of willows, and a bell hanging on a rope from a branch.

"Do we ring the bell?" asked Simon.

Father Sam shook his head.

"There'd be no point. The bell's for the ferry. But there can be no ferry so long as the Middle Mere is iced over. What we have to discover is, will the ice bear us?"

Simon pried a sizable rock from the side of the track and hurled it as far as he was able onto the ice. Nothing happened.

"But one rock isn't as heavy as two horses and five people and a sedan chair."

"And two bears," said Dido. "And a flock of sheep."

"Send the bears out," said Father Sam. "See if the ice will bear them." He laughed heartily at his own joke, but Simon was scandalized.

"Why put *them* at risk? They didn't ask to be sent to this country. I'll go."

"No, no, my boy, that would not do," Father Sam said hastily. "You are next in succession to the throne. Harry had better go."

"I can't swim," grumbled Harry.

"I'll go," snapped Dido, who found this discussion a silly waste of time. "I swim like a herring—though let's hope I don't need to."

She set out with caution on the ice, which, under a couple of inches of snow, was extremely slippery. And, once she was fairly out in the channel, away from sheltering banks and thickets, the wind, icy and buffeting, made it hard to keep upright.

Peering ahead, she saw clumps of rush and snow-covered islets. And, from time to time, between gusts of snow, she had a glimpse of the high-arched monastery

225

buildings climbing the steep slope on the far side of the channel. To her right the high silhouette of the viaduct appeared and disappeared in the storm. Somewhere down there, under the ice, between those tall stone legs, lay a shattered carriage and four horses and some drowned people. A grim thought. Not that any of 'em's much loss, thought Dido. Lot and Jorinda—what a pair! And the two old gals—one of 'em at least as bent as a buckle. The duchess was certainly no angel and t'other one, according to Simon, seemed to have been playing both ends against the middle.

Now, rounding an islet sprouted over with frozen willow wands, she could see her way clear ahead. This was probably the main channel, where the current would be strongest and the ice was likely to be thinnest. Wish I had a pair of skates, thought Dido. She remembered a winter in London when the Thames had frozen, and in Rose Alley where she lived there had been only one pair of skates among seventy children. Belonged to Sindy Rogers, the ironmonger's kid, but she let us all have a go. Didn't take long to learn. Hey, there's a feller in black a-waving on the far shore. Does he mean yes, it's all rug, come along? Or does he mean go back, the ice won't hold ye? Well, I'm a-going and hope for the best. If the ice won't hold, he can blame well jump in and haul me out.

But the ice did hold. And in another five minutes Dido was safe on the farther bank, having her hands enthusiastically shaken by a long-legged lad in monk's robes,

226

who cried, "Welcome! Welcome to the Priory! Welcome indeed! Father Mistigris would be here himself to welcome you, but a ship has foundered on the seaward side of Otherland Bank and all the brothers are down there helping to rescue the crew. But I see there are others of your party. . . . Do you want to signal them to come, now we know the ice will carry them?"

Dido said dubiously, "One of 'em's the king. And he's sick, in a great clumsy carry-chair. And there's a pair of bears. And two horses . . . and a flock of sheep. I dunno if 'twill be safe to fetch the king across in that contraption; it's mighty heavy. But he's awful sick and like to die."

"I'll fetch a stretcher from the barn," said the boy. "I'm Brother Mark, by the way. We quite often get sick people coming here." He disappeared, running toward a stone, thatched building, and came back in a minute with two poles and a canvas sheath. Meanwhile the sheep had decided, on their own initiative, to amble across and were now mustering hopefully outside the barn. "Yes, go in, go in," Brother Mark absently told them. "There's plenty hay inside." And the flock at once did so. "Now let us cross and get your friends."

Mark had also brought out two pairs of skates made from deer's antlers. He passed a pair to Dido, who gratefully put them on.

"Say, thanks, Mark, that'll make a power of difference."

The skates did indeed make a difference, and they were

227

able to cross the channel in a few minutes. The party on the other shore had seen the stretcher and waited.

"That was well thought of, Mark," said Father Sam. "I doubt the sedan would be too heavy. But I trust that our royal friend, wrapped in his quilts on the stretcher, will take no harm if the crossing be done as fast as possible."

With everybody helping, the exchange was made and the king, wrapped in coverings, was borne across the channel by Simon and Father Sam, wearing the skates. Mark brought the king's bag of needments; Dido and Harry led the horses, who slid and whickered nervously on the ice and were kept at a safe distance behind the sick man in case their weight proved too much. The bears followed independently, studying the ice as if they hoped to find fish under it.

"Brother Isaac will take care of them," called Mark. "He is a great fisherman. Now I fear we have to climb three hundred steps."

The bears and horses were left in the barn, and the rest of the party took turns carrying the stretcher up the steps, which was far more arduous than the trip over the frozen channel.

"It is because of floods and pirates," panted Mark as they approached the great arched doorway that led into the monastery courtyard. "Floods never rise as high as this, and pirates climb so slowly that everybody has time to hide."

He led them through some very untidy cloisters and past the Priory chapel to a big bare community chamber with a view of the sea through large unglazed windows. Dido gasped as she looked from one of these; the drop on the seaward side of Otherland Mount was sheer — three hundred feet down to the tossing waves below. Far to her left she could see the curve of the great shingle bank running round to Wan Hope Point. And, between gusts of snow, she could also see a ship rolling and pitching, slewed over on her side, half smothered by huge white waves that came galloping in toward the hostile shore. Tiny black figures on the beach were hauling on ropes from the ship, but their efforts seemed puny compared with the might of the elements. The sea's roar could be heard, even from this height, and the scream of the wind.

Mark shook his head. "They can probably rescue the crew," he said, "but I'm afraid the ship is done for."

"I don't see many monks down there," said Dido.

"There are only nine of us left now. But come this way and I'll show you the guest chambers and the kitchen."

The guest chambers were a row of little rooms, probably monks' cells, on the landward side of the Priory. And just as well too, thought Dido, or the guests would hardly get a wink of sleep with the sea roaring away like it is. On the steep hillside running down to the Middle Mere, there grew massive trees, forest oaks, ilex and sycamore; their boughs heaved and swung in the gale, but they protected this side of the Priory from the worst of the tempest. Here the king was installed in a quiet little room with a narrow white bed. While Simon and

Harry were attending him, Mark said to Dido, "Come and I'll show you the kitchen and you can brew up something hot for the poor old gentleman. Matthew, the kitchen brother, is down at the wreck, but Brother Isaac, the cellarer, will show you where to find things."

The kitchen, farther along on the same side of the building, was a large room, almost completely bare, with little to show its function except for some holes in the stone wall containing a pile of earthenware bowls, and a fireplace that held a pile of gray ash with one red spark.

"Brother Isaac will be down below in the pantry."

Dido was anxious to check out the pantry, as she could see nothing in the kitchen that would provide a hot drink for the king. Mark led her down a steep flight of steps to a room that seemed to be cut out of the hillside below the kitchen. It had holes for windows looking out onto the big trees and the Middle Mere, and more steps led out to kitchen gardens, orchards and dairies. It was also most satisfactorily furnished with piles of root vegetables, strings of onions and herbs, great earthenware vats of milk, barrels of cider, cheeses and sacks of grain and flour. Dried fish hung in bunches. Dido, who had learned to make chowder while on board a whaling ship, helped herself to onions, potatoes, milk, butter, dried parsley and bay leaves, fish and peppercorns.

"You got any dried salt pork?" she asked Mark. But he shook his head.

"We are vegetarians—except for the fish," he said.

"I'll manage without, then."

Now Brother Isaac came climbing up the stair from the kitchen gardens. Dido could see why he was not out with the others rescuing the shipwrecked sailors, for he was desperately lame, could only just drag himself along sideways. It did not seem to trouble him; he was a cheerful little man and beamed at Dido.

"You need a box to work on," he said. "Mark'll find ye a box."

It seemed the kitchen was furnished with boxes and bits of timber salvaged from shipwrecks, which were later burned up for firewood. There had not been a wreck for some time and the supply was running low, but Isaac said cheerfully, "Plenty coming now! Not that we mean harm to the crew, don't think it!" he added. "But they are Burgundians, after all, come to invade our country, so if they get wrecked, they have only themselves to thank."

"Oh, so it's a Burgundian ship?"

"Yes, my lovey, they all speak Burgundy French, and they will be asking for beef stew and red wine, which we don't have. But Sir Thomas will see to it that they all get sent home again."

Dido had not the least idea who Sir Thomas might be, nor did she care. Mark found her a wooden packing case that had contained candles; on this she chopped up onions, fish, potatoes, celery, herbs, then added beans and corn. She blew up the kitchen fire with some kindling supplied by Brother Isaac and set a nourishing soup to simmer.

Brother Isaac said, "I'd help ye, but I can see that ye are

231

managing just fine without my interference, and I'm all behind with my praying; there's extra prayers required for those poor souls on the ship, and then there's the sick man in the guest room—did ye say he was the king? Ah, then he'll need a deal of praying, I reckon, to smooth his way into the next world—not that I ever heard any harm of the poor gentleman, but he must have a whole pack of cares on his shoulders. And my prayers take twice as long as the other brothers', for I can't kneel, with my infirmity, so I have to manage on a prayer frame that Brother Mark made me. Eh, he's a handy young fellow, so he is."

The prayer frame was a triangular structure, padded with sheep's wool.

" 'Tis becoming a bit bald, the padding. I need more wool, so I do."

"We brought some sheep," Dido said. "You're welcome to their wool. I'm sure Simon will agree. I dunno where he picked up the sheep."

Brother Isaac was delighted to hear about the sheep. " 'Tis blankets I'll be weaving for all the brothers."

While her soup was simmering over the kitchen fire, Dido went along to see how the king was settling. She found him restless and fretful. Simon had gone down to the beach to help the rescuers and old Harry had fallen into exhausted sleep.

"Where is Titania?" pleaded the king. "Where is my coronet? I want to go home! I want to go home. I don't belong here; I don't belong."

Dido wondered sadly where he did belong; what place

232

was it that he thought of as *home*? Certainly it could not be this bare and windy monastery.

"When can I catch the train to King's Cross? Why don't I hear any nightingales?"

"*Dear* Uncle King, I don't reckon there's a-going to be a many nightingales here, so close to the sea. Can't you make do with seagulls? There's a plenty of *them*."

"I want to go home!"

"We're all going home," Dido improvised.

"We are? When? When?"

"When we come to our journey's end!"

For some reason this reply seemed to satisfy the king, and he lay silent for a while, clasping Dido's hand.

In a very low voice, she sang him one of her father's songs:

> "*When does the wind go home?*
> *When he has swept the sky*
> *And pushed the clouds into corners*
> *And hung them up to dry . . .*"

She saw Simon peering round the door and tiptoed out to him.

"The old feller's gone to sleep. . . . Why is he so set on having nightingales?"

They moved a little way down the passage. Simon said, "Aunt Titania, the old lady who looked after him lately, she foretold that he would hear nightingales singing before his death."

233

"She was one of the two who got killt in that carriage?"

"Yes. I always thought she loved the king. I'd never dreamed that she was in some way connected with Baron Magnus, with Lot and the duchess. Perhaps her story about nightingales was a lie . . . to encourage him to stay alive till that other fellow with a Saxon name came from the north. . . . Poor Cousin Dick!"

"Or maybe she went to spy on them all at Fogrum Hall, see what they were up to. I guess we'll never know," said Dido.

"She must have meant to come back to Darkwater when she packed the king's bag of needments. I see she put her own embroidery things in as well. I don't suppose you do embroidery, Dido, do you? You wouldn't have a use for them?"

She shook her head. "Learned to knit, I did, aboard the whaler. But I'm no hand with a needle."

"She also packed this thing among the embroidery silks. What do you think it is?"

Simon had in his hand a small convoluted object made of ivory.

"Oh, I know what that is," said Dido. "My aunt Tinty had one. It's a hearing aid. But the king's not deaf, is he? He seems to hear all that's going on. I wonder if it works." She fitted the object into her ear and exclaimed, "My stars!"

"What's up?"

Simon tried it and was equally startled. "I can hear birds singing!"

"Hey!" said Dido. "I'll lay you a gross of guineas those are nightingales!"

Simon and Dido stared at each other.

"She was going to fool him—when the time came," Dido said.

"How wicked!"

"Do you think she meant to *kill* him?"

"When the right moment came, perhaps. She had been giving him some drug in his food that made him see ghosts. But she needed to have the archbishop of Wessex at hand—and he's dead, poor old boy, killed by Magnus's people."

"Yes, Father Sam told me. I saw him, old Whitgift, only a few days ago; he wanted me to find the king . . . and you, 'cos you're the next in line. Is that really so, Simon?"

"Well, I believe so," he said gloomily. "Though old Aunt Titania did seem to have this other candidate up her sleeve, somebody called Aelfric of Bernicia. But he seems to have been kept away by bad weather."

Father Sam joined them, wet and exhausted from helping with the wreck.

"Well, we got them ashore, all ninety-nine of them," he said cheerfully. "All but the captain—he would stay by his ship, silly fellow. They are all in the warming room, drying off, and Brother Matthew says your chowder is done, Miss Dido, and may he move it off the fire so he can brew the Burgundians something hot? Father Mistigris has gone off to send for Sir Thomas."

Dido went to rescue her chowder. Simon said, "Who is Sir Thomas? What does he have to do with the shipwrecked sailors?"

"Sir Thomas Coldacre. He and the duchess of Burgundy made the arrangements to fetch all these Burgundians here; so he can just take charge of them now," said Father Sam.

"Sir Thomas will have to be told that his granddaughter is dead."

"I doubt if he'll grieve much for her, poor silly girl. Nor for Lothar, who was never anything but bad news. The duchess wanted to put Lot on the throne, but that would have been *really* disastrous. You'll make a better job of it, my boy."

"But," said Simon reluctantly, "even if I do have to take on the job, we can't go ahead or do anything without the new archbishop of Wessex—and who in the world is that? Maybe there isn't one. How could there be?"

"Oh, that's no problem," said Father Sam cheerfully. "It's meself."

"*You*, Father Sam?"

" 'Twas the king's job to appoint me, and he did that. I came top of the list of six chosen by the Convocation of Wessex Clergy last month. All we need now, to carry out the requirements of the succession ritual, is the coronet itself. I dare say old Lady Titania was hunting for it when she went off to visit the duchess at Fogrum; there had been a rumor that it was left in Lady Adelaide's desk."

"No, it wasn't there," said Simon. "Dido told me. She happened to look in the desk and all she found was a diary. And Fogrum Hall is burned down now, so if the coronet was there, it's gone for good."

"Well, well. Perhaps it will turn up here," Father Sam said hopefully. "After all, Alfred himself was here, hiding from the Vikings, in the year 878, and left the monks a charter to prove it. I'll ask Father Mistigris when I see him. Now I had best go back to those poor Burgundian fellows, who are quite shocked and exhausted. They'll know better another time, if they are asked to invade someone else's country. . . ."

He strode away, dripping, and Simon returned to the king, who said piteously, "Simon! I want to go home!"

chapter seventeen

A PIGEON FLUTTERED out of the sky and landed on Simon's shoulder. He and Dido were at the foot of three hundred stairs, looking out across the frozen mere.

"All the birds and beasts take a rare shine to you these days, Simon," said Dido.

"It's since I stopped eating meat. Can be a bit inconvenient at times."

He carefully undid the paper wrapped in silk, which had been wrapped round the pigeon's leg. "This was probably meant for Aunt Titania. She had a messenger service." He read the words on the paper and frowned in perplexity. "No. It seems to be *from* Aunt Titania—must have been written before she died."

"Maybe the pigeon got lost in the storm. Who's it to?"

"I don't know. Me, perhaps. Or the king."

"What's it say?"

"It says: 'I was wrong about Chaucer. He adapted the lines from a local poet, Gregory Pollard of Wan Hope: *"And bye the Middel Mere, Oft ye may heare Midwinter Nightingale to human eares tell out Hyr Piteous Tale."* 'I' Plantagenet.'"

"What does it mean?"

"I don't *know*," said Simon crossly. Here was yet another puzzle that needed solving, and he was already so tired he thought he could go to sleep for a hundred years—if he ever had the chance to start. "Poor old king," he said. "He told me he wanted to die at Darkwater because he'd been a boy there. And the nightingales . . . But we couldn't leave him there with the flood coming."

"And Alfred's crown wasn't there?"

"No," Simon said. "I have had a really thorough search. I just pray that it's here somewhere. He might have left it here sometime for safekeeping."

"There's an awful lot of places to look," said Dido. She stared up at the high stone walls and ruined arches on the hillside above them. A thousand years ago this place had been a thriving community. King Alfred had been here hiding from the Norsemen and granted it a charter. Even two hundred years ago there had been two hundred monks, growing corn and vegetables, making cider from the apples. But now there were only nine. Brother Mark was the last novice to apply and it did not seem likely that there would be any to follow him.

"It's a bit sad," shivered Dido, looking out across the frozen Mere.

They were waiting for Sir Thomas Coldacre to arrive. And then they would have to break the news to him that his granddaughter and stepgrandson were both dead.

"That Jorinda," said Dido cautiously, "she was a rum sort of gal."

"Hasty in her actions."

"Had you known her long? Met her, maybe, when I was in Ameriky?"

"No. I just met her on the train a few days ago."

"She said you and she were a-going to get married."

"She was wrong. There was not the slightest chance of that."

"I reckon that's just as well. She wouldn't have been right for you."

"The only person I've met so far," said Simon, "who would be right for me is you, Dido."

She shook her head. "Not if you're a-going to be king, Simon. I'd *never* do as queen, never! Not me. It's too high a step from Rose Alley to Saint Jim's Palace. You'll have to look for someone classier. Or turn down the job."

"I don't think I can do that," he said unhappily. "Then it'll have to be no one at all."

"Maybe they can find somebody else to put on their throne. Maybe Cousin Alf will turn up yet from Burnham-on-Sea. . . ."

"Here comes Sir Thomas," said Simon, squinting across the ice. "He seems to have brought a whole load of luggage with him."

Sir Thomas had ridden to the Middle Mere on a

weight-carrying hunter, escorted by his man Gribben on another, with a massive quantity of clothes and provisions, including a side of ham and a barrel of liquor. But they had come to a halt on the far side of the channel and, dismounting, surveyed the ice doubtfully.

Simon and Dido walked across to greet them.

"Good day, sir," said Simon. "I'm Simon Battersea, staying here at present with His Majesty, who is—who is in poor health. And this is Dido Twite."

"How do," said Sir Thomas. "Battersea, eh? I used to know your uncle and aunt at Loose Chippings. Rattling fast country around there, and your uncle kept a doocid good pack of hounds. Battersea, hey? You sent me a check for my sheep. More than dismal old Minna of Burgundy ever did."

"Why, yes," said Simon. "Those sheep were being disgracefully ill treated. But they are now in the care of the monks here, who will keep them for their wool and are happy to have them. The sheep are happy too. I am not so sure about the bears."

"Bears, *bears*? I never ordered bears. *Boots*, it should have been, electric boots."

"I understand from the monks," said Simon, "that a consignment of boots was washed ashore last week from a wrecked Russian cargo ship. But the electric elements didn't work. Soaking in the water, you know. The monks gave them to the poor. There were a few bears as well who swam to shore. . . ."

"Pesky Burgundians!" said Sir Thomas. "I didn't

know the *king* was here. I've come about some godfor-saken Burgundians, got washed up here, I understand, fetched over by that conniving Minna of Burgundy so as to put her no-account nevvy on the throne. But *he's* stuck his spoon in the wall, so I hear, and no loss to anybody — he was my stepgrandson, and a *devilish* cub since he could crawl — and now I hear the Burgundians have stove in their vessel on Querck Bank — so it's said, that right? So I've had all my trouble and expense for noth-ing, curse them all for a pigeon-brained cack-handed set of blunderheads!"

"I'm afraid you are rightly informed," said Simon. "Baron Magnus and his son are both dead. The baron died in the fire at Fogrum Hall and his son and the duchess fell off the viaduct."

"Was Lothar drunk?"

"Yes. And before that he had inadvertently killed his sister by stabbing her with a Saxon spear." Simon did not add that the killing stroke had been meant for him.

"Eh, dear me. Poor Jorinda. Poor lass. But she was a flighty one, like her mother before her. I knew it'd be only a matter of time before she came to no good. So I've had all my trouble for nothing — importing Russian bears and electric boots. To tell ye the truth I'm just as glad to keep King Dick on the throne. But now — hmnnn? I've come to pay off the Burgundians and I reckon to pass the night in the Priory, for it'll be dark in an hour or two. But how to get my cattle across and a few odds and bits for the night? I take it the monks can furnish me with a room?"

"Oh, yes, there are plenty of rooms," said Simon. "And I think it will be safe enough if we bring over your luggage piece by piece."

Accordingly this was done. Sir Thomas walked over first. "Seventeen stone!" he confided to Dido. "Give or take a pound or two. 'Pon my sainted saddlebag! Am I expected to climb up that unending staircase?"

Dido, however, had found a diagonal approach to the warming chamber, where the shipwrecked Burgundians were accommodated, and she took Sir Thomas that way, which was not so steep as the stair, and there were trees to hold on to. Meanwhile Simon and Gribben brought over the two horses and the provisions in a series of trips.

"Fortunate thing!" Sir Thomas explained to Dido as they slowly climbed. "M'granddaughter helped me answer and send off a confounded chain-letter affair — which *I* thought a load of pernicious rubbish, but it has paid off uncommonly well. Money comes in every mail, left me quite plump in the pocket; so I can give those Burgundian rogues enough journey money to send them back to Burgundy. Best thing to do, the way matters have turned out."

"You pay them to go home?" said Dido. "That's mighty obliging of you, Sir T."

"Generally works out best that way. Danegeld, you know."

Dido left Sir Thomas in the warming chamber, talking and giving orders to the shipwrecked Burgundians (luckily their English was far better than his French), and went up to the king's little room. Father Sam and Father Mistigris were there, and Simon arrived soon after.

"Sir Thomas Coldacre would like to come and pay his respects to the king," he said. "Is His Majesty strong enough to meet a stranger, do you think?"

"He is growing weaker all the time," said Father Sam in a low worried voice. "I don't know —"

But the king had caught Simon's words.

"Sir Thomas Coldacre?" he whispered. "Nay, he's no stranger. I ken him well. Fine I'd like tae see the callant! Many's the braw run he and I took togither after some canny farrant fox, and many's the grand gaedown and flagon of doch-and-doris we shared togither in those same days. Bring the auld loon in; I'd like fine to have a crack wi' him."

Father Sam and Simon gazed at each other in amazement. It was a long time since they had heard the king speak so strongly and so connectedly.

Simon went off and soon returned with Sir Thomas, who subsided, creaking, on one knee and kissed the king's hand.

"Sorry I am to see you in such poor shape, sir. But there! I reckon we all come to the end of the run sooner or later. And you're in good hands, I see; Father Sam is as shrewd as any sawbones, and the monks with Father

244

Mistigris here can surely give ye a fine rousing send-off. But still it grieves me to see ye brought so low. Do ye remember that run we had over Sheeplow Water Meadows when Puffington headed the fox and the huntsman was soused in a clay hole? Lord bless me, how we laughed!"

"Ay, well I mind it," whispered the king. "And the whips all got left ahind! Those were the days, mon, those were the days!"

"Now, Dickie man, is there aught I can do for ye? Messages I can take to folk for ye? Bills paid, mortgages redeemed, aught of that sort? I just paid off all those Burgundian mercenaries, ye'll be glad to hear; the silly lubbers can't wait to get on the next packet home. . . ."

"Nay, there's naught, I thank ye," whispered the king. "Auld Aunt Titania's gone afore me; I felt it in my hairt two-three hours agone. All I maun do now is wait for death—but waiting's a sad, unchancy business, forbye! 'Tis like waiting for a dismal bink of a train that never comes. Do ye think," he suddenly said to Dido, who was standing at the end of his bed, "Dido, dearest girl, do ye think we'll likewise be obleeged to wait, to wait for meals or trains or meetings in the waurld to come?"

"Croopus, *no,* Your Majesty," Dido said firmly. "*Nobody* waits for *anything* there!"

"Well answered, my dearie! I'm blythe tae hear that. Ay—come to think—there is *one* thing ye can do to obleege me," the king said, turning back to Sir Thomas. "This coronet ceremony—King Alfred's headpiece—ye ken? We're a' waiting for that, and sair fashed, for the coronet's no' to hand; we hae the archbishop here, and the successor yonder"—he pointed at Simon—"but wheer's the cockermoney with which to crown him? Do ye ken wheer it might be, Sir Tammas?"

"Why, yes," said Sir Thomas, sounding a little surprised, "I see it right there."

He pointed. "The Lady Adelaide used to be good friends with my daughter, Zoe, at one time, and the Lady A was always a great one for embroidery; she was forever making kneelers for Clarion Wells cathedral or some such ploy. She'd long been friends with the prince of Wales (as you were then, sir) before she married him—you. And, one time, you lent her that coronet for an embroidery frame; she told us that. You must have lent it to her again after your own crowning. Do ye remember now?"

All eyes turned to Aunt Titania's needlework equipment, which was lying in a muddle on a wooden stool. Dido went over slowly and picked up the piece of embroidered linen, which was pulled tight over a circular embroidery hoop. She undid the hoop—which was in fact two hoops, one tight inside the other—separated them and dropped the embroidered cloth on the floor. The inner hoop, which had been concealed under the cloth, was made of twisted dark copper studded here and there with pale green peridots.

"Ay, yon's the biggonet," said the king contentedly. "Well I kenned it wad be certain tae come tae light somewhere. And I'm much obleeged tae ye, Tam, auld friend! Now, let us hirple through this fashous ceremony and hae done with it. Father Sam, are ye there?"

Father Sam, whose eyes had been nearly starting out of their sockets during the previous few minutes, moved forward, took the coronet from Dido and handed it to the king, retaining one side of it.

"Kneel down," he said to Simon, who silently did so, close to the king's bed.

Dido, standing by Sir Thomas at the end of the bed, noticed that the gale outside had stopped blowing. The room was quite silent.

Father Sam said some Latin words, quite a long string of them. Then he put the copper circlet on Simon's head. Then he waited a few minutes. Then he added a few more Latin words. Dido heard something that sounded like *"Ubi non praevenit rem desiderium"* but Dido knew no Latin. Then he said, "You may stand up now, my boy. That's it."

Simon stood up. Then they all heard, quite distinctly, a loud blast of dazzling song outside the window. Birds, fluting, sizzling, twittering, jug-jugging, singing their heads off.

"Nightingales," whispered the king contentedly. "It must be Saint Lucy's Day."

Then he died.

"Oh, confound it!" exclaimed Sir Thomas, scrambling to his feet. "I was just about to fetch my brandy-warmer—Gribben had unpacked it—and give the old fellow a snort of red-hot aquavit—cockadoodle broth—brandy beaten up with eggs. That would have roused him! Now it's too late. Too late! But how about you, my boy? (Should address you as Your Majesty, I suppose, but it's a bit early to start that.) Would you care for a nip of the old stingo? Or you, Miss Dido?" Simon shook his head.

And Dido, crying her heart out on the floor at the end of the bed, made no reply.

About the Author

JOAN AIKEN is the daughter of the American poet Conrad Aiken. Born in England, in Rye, Sussex, she was educated at home by her mother until the age of twelve, when she attended Wychwood, a small progressive boarding school in Oxford. She began working for the BBC at an early age; she was librarian in charge of documents for the United Nations London Information Centre, served as features editor at *Argosy* magazine and had a brief stint as an advertising copywriter before turning her hand to writing full-time.

Joan Aiken is the author of more than a hundred books for adults and young readers. Her novels are acclaimed internationally. A Mystery Writers of America Award winner, she is also the recipient of the *Guardian* Award for children's literature for three books: the classic *The Wolves of Willoughby Chase* (for which she also won the Lewis Carroll Award), *Nightbirds on Nantucket* and *Black Hearts in Battersea*. She was recently named a Member of the Order of the British Empire by Queen Elizabeth II.

Joan Aiken is the mother of a daughter and a son; she lives in Sussex, England.